Tides of the

Kennebec

Tides of the

Kennebec

Kathleen Vellenga

40 PRESS

Cover photo and book design by John Toren

Forty Press, LLC
427 Van Buren Street
Anoka, MN 55303
www.fortypress.com

ISBN 978-1-938473-34-0

To my true friends, through bright times and dim;
Ruthena Fink and Terrie Brandt

Author's note

To learn how to write stories, I first listened. Thanks to my story-telling family, as I child I soaked up stories, including about when my grandparents arrived in Nebraska, replacing the original Lakota people. The world came to our family in mountain-time Nebraska, including dinner guests who were Americans of Japanese descent who'd been ripped from their families in California and deposited in a camp near my hometown.

As I grew up, I told my own stories, sometimes embellishing a little. While volunteering at a maternal-infant care clinic and with diverse children in my congregation, I listened to people whose stories were different from mine. Friendships with people who initially would not look me in the eye were my reward. When I was elected to public office, I found that campaigning, as well as persuading colleagues, involved my willingness to listen to others' stories as well as to tell my own.

Elizabeth Tilley and John Howland caught my eye when I found a book on the Mayflower in my father's library. Elizabeth was orphaned at thirteen and married John Howland two years later; a story that stayed in my heart. What caused a young woman to marry a man twice her age? I did not want to let the historical record be the only story.

Knowing that both Howlands would have believed the Wampanoag people were "savages," I knew I had to create Wampanoag characters to carry their own story. This would not have been possible without many Indigenous people here in Minnesota, Massachusetts, and Maine.

Having procured a patente for Kenebeck, they now erected a house up above in ye river in ye most convenientest place for trade, as they conceived, and furnished the same with comodities for yt end, both winter & somer, not only with corne, but also with such other commodities as ye fishermen had traded with them, as coats, shirts, ruggs, & blankets, biskett, pease, prunes, &c.; and what they could not have out of England, they bought of the fishing ships, and so carried on their bussines as well as they could.

– From "Of Plimoth Plantation" by William Bradford

And strange it was to see the great allteration it made in a few years amonge ye Indeans them selves; for all the Indeans of these parts, & ye Massachussets, had none or very litle of it, but ye sachems & some spetiall persons that wore a litle of it for ornamente. Only it was made & kepte amonge ye Nariganssets, & Pequents, which grew rich & potent by it, and these people were poore & begerly, and had no use of it. But after it grue thus to be a comoditie in these parts, these Indeans fell into it allso, and to learne how to make it; for ye Narigansets doe geather ye shells of which yey make it from their shors. And it hath now continued a current comoditie aboute this 20. years, and it may prove a drugg in time.

– From "Of Plimoth Plantation" by William Bradford

The English who first came to this country were but a handful of people, forlorn, poor and distressed. My father relieved their distresses in the most kind and hospitable manner. He gave them land to plant and build upon...they flourished and increased...by various means they got possessed of a great part of his territory. But he still remained their friend 'til he died. My elder brother became sachem. They pretended to suspect him of evil designs against them. He was seized and confined and thereby thrown into illness and died. Soon after I became sachem, they disarmed all my people...our lands were taken. But a small part of the dominion of my ancestors remains. I am determined not to live until I have no country.

– Statement by Metacom (King Phillip) at the beginning of the Wampanoag revolt. "Preamble to a declaration of war...a mournful summary of accumulated wrongs." Samuel Arnold.

1

1628
PLIMOTH PLANTATION
MASSACHUSETTS BAY COLONY

Elisabeth Tilley Howland:

"Standish says that whenever we're not in Maine, the trading with the Abenaki falls prey to poachers," John sighed. This was an old, troubling tale we had discussed many times since he started going to Maine. "Nothing has changed, it only gets worse," he said, his voice raising. "Bloody gentry in England keep sending a scurrilous lot of thieves to steal beaver and timber from our territory. We have trading rights!"

The greed he described did not surprise me. It was as common among men as flies above a milk bucket. The richer they are, the more they want. We lived in constant anxiety, knowing our entire planation would be back under King Charles' rule if we did not pay our debts.

"How is Standish planning to prevent this?" I asked.

John smiled wryly, for our captain was known more for bravery than for strategy.

"Will he lead an army up there, then?" I asked, with more accuracy.

John took a breath. "Nay, he wants me—us—to lead a contingent to live in Maine long enough to enforce the truce between Plimoth Plantation and the Abenaki."

"Us?"

"Yea, us."

"Me? Our children? Live there?" I had a feeling of snakes writhing in my gut.

He glanced about our little house. It was only one room, a hearth on one wall, our bed on another. With a table in between, a bench for the children and me, and John's chair, leaving barely enough space for the children to spread their blankets on the floor at night. "We've already built a fort. We will have rooms there. At least we would be together."

"I admit that I long for you every day you're gone," I said. That was an understatement.

John had been taking these trips north for four years, ever since our leaders negotiated trading rights with the Abenaki tribes. The children did not understand his responsibility, but they felt his absence, as did I. The weeks he was gone were long and dreary. During the day, I depended on others to keep the firewood split, the water lugged. At least we now had a grist mill on the creek and I no longer had to pound grain.

The worst day was better than any night. When dark fell and I was left alone with my children, I often thought I could not bear one more night. Even when the children left their blankets on the floor and crawled into bed with me, I slept fitfully. Waking from a dream, I still seemed to smell John's scent, feel his warmth. The reality of my empty bed chilled me, the knowledge that only God knew if my husband would return safely. In Maine I would not be in an empty bed and the children would be with their father.

Over the years, I had grown accustomed to John's responsibilities. To manage our resources, Plimoth Plantation was divided into two companies, both of which used the labor and goods of the households in each company. This efficiency provided an increased source for repayment to the investors. John was named leader of one company, which I privately admitted to him made me proud. We prayed for humility and that his leadership would successfully bring in the resources to finally pay off our debt. This venture in Maine was essential. But moving there was far different than seasonal trips to the Kennebec River.

My questions spilled out: "What is winter like up north?" "Do any other Christians live there?" "Who else will go?" "Who will lead us?"

"It will be not much worse than here, a bit colder and more snow." John stood in our open door. "Yea, others from my company will go with us. I will be in charge in Maine. It will be quiet there and we would not be surrounded by all these new people. Ye would be free from the spying and gossip by those who see Satan in the least thing." He came to me, sat and took my left hand—no need to remind me of the accusations of witchcraft brought by my willful bad hand.

"But my friends are here, not just those who spread rumors. Who else will go?"

"John and Priscilla Alden, and their brood. A few other men." John paused. "And Black Whale."

"Will Attitash go?"

"I have to persuade thee to come, my love, before I inquire after Attitash."

Was he really giving me a choice?

"What if ye can't persuade me, John?"

"Then I would have to live there without thee for a year or two—until the trading is secure." John paused, tears filled his eyes. "I do not want to leave. It breaks my heart that I would make thee leave everyone and everything ye know." He wiped his eyes with his sleeve and held me close a long moment. "We have a choice—but both choices are bad. I go alone and we live far apart until this can be settled, or ye and the children come with me."

"But ye could become accustomed to being apart." I tried

to appear mature, stoic, the kind of wife who perseveres despite what God demands of us.

"Accustomed? It would be more than I could bear!" His green eyes showed a sudden darkness. "Would it not be the same for thee? Or do ye prefer the comfort of home to being with me in a strange place?"

"Is my choice only to go with thee or stay? Could someone else go?"

John pulled me close. "I must go. I have been chosen to be the leader."

I snuggled into his shoulder. My own tears slid down my cheeks and melted on his shirt.

"I know ye enjoy more civilized conditions here," John said. "The grist mill, the village oven, cows, sheep, even horses."

"The horse is thine; I've yet to learn to ride."

"But ye shall ride soon." John smiled, knowing I was taking my time getting acquainted with the fearsome beast he rode upon so happily.

"And I shall miss our oven—only since our little John was born do we get to bake bread in the oven. I shall have to go back to making bread in the skillet."

"Did ye say, 'shall,'?"

"I mean I have to." The horse and oven were the least of it. "What if Attitash doesn't go?"

"If it pleases thee to go, I think Attitash will too." John sighed. "'Tis a hard thing. But we *shall* come back home to live in Plimoth, that I promise thee."

There was little time to be nostalgic for the only home I'd known since my parents brought me on the Mayflower. Plimoth then was just decaying Indian huts and plowed fields. Anything on dry land was acceptable to us. Even with the heartbreak—my family and so many others dying that first winter, the curse inflicted on me by the Cur, and all the trauma we survived since. I loved our little house. I loved the sea and the hills. This was home.

2

Elisabeth:

Attitash came to Plimoth a week after I learned we must move to Maine. Her young son was with her and we sat on the bench outside my door as the children played.

"Some of my elders don't think we should go with you." Attitash said.

This was not a surprise. I'd been aware since Black Whale first accompanied my husband on trips to the Kennebec River that many of the Wampanoag elders opposed our going there at all, much less to live there. Black Whale told John that the Wampanoag thought their own trading with the Abenaki was sufficient and that they need not risk their relationship with the Abenaki by linking with our plantation's need.

"Do ye and Black Whale understand that the bad men from Boston are dealing for so many of the pelts trapped by the Abenaki that there are not even enough for Wampanoag?" I asked. "These thieves encroach on your territory as well as the Abenaki's."

My son, young John, and Attitash's son, Mosk, were tossing a ball made of rags. Their laughter turned to shrieks when the dogs ran off with the rag ball. Attitash and I smiled at the boys' attempts to chase the dogs. Our families had been friends for twelve years. I wondered if Attitash and Black Whale could move their family away from their own tribe. It might be even more difficult than for our family. We had helped Attitash's people and they had helped us, but they could be ready to give up on us. Still, we could not succeed in Maine without our friends. I drew a deep breath, pushing down the fear. "Without thee and Black Whale to speak to the Abenaki in their words, the poachers—the bad men—will drive us and our friends out," I told Attitash. "Will ye go with us?"

"I will think on it and talk to my elders, Esapett."

I bit my tongue. Why couldn't their king, Massasowet and his men ever make a decision without waiting for the old women? We would have to leave soon or cold weather would jeopardize our journey. I leaned against a tree, feeling as though the ground was shifting beneath me. There was so much at stake—and too many complicating attitudes among both our own people in Plimoth and our Indian friends. Would it ever get any better?

The boys came racing back, ball in hand, dogs yapping at their feet.

"Quit playing and go carry wood to the house," I scolded my son.

Attitash:

As Esapett and I watched our sons play together happily, I told her that my mother wondered why our families should go to live with the Abenaki. "Mama and Grandmother listened and agreed to think about this request before taking it to the Grandmothers' Council," I said. "Did your grandmothers across the Big Salt Water tell you why they need so many pelts?"

Elisabeth's eyebrows raised, her cheeks reddened. "My grandmothers were long ago called to the Lord. Even my mother is not alive."

I was not sure what she meant. Had all the Strangers' grandmothers gone on their spirit journey?

Our boys continued to play as she tried to explain why her people needed Black Whale and me to go with them. "We don't speak Algonquin, we need your words to trade. And we need the trade," Esapett's voice lost its usual gentle tone. Beads of sweat broke out on the back of my neck. Esapett was usually so calm and friendly. If she was afraid, that meant her people were in danger. And if they were in danger, my people were in greater danger. Our boys came running back, laughing and pushing each other. I saw young Jon-owland playfully pointing a firestick at my son. I rolled my shoulders to shake off the vision of my real encounter with one not long ago. Esapett barked at her son to go help gather wood and left with him.

Mosk asked, "Why did Esapett speak so crossly to Young-John?"

"She is a worried mother," I told my son. He asked what worried her, and I told him, adding, "We might be going to the Abenaki with Esapett's family."

Mosk's mouth opened wide in astonishment. "Why would we go there?"

"To help our friends."

"Why don't Esapett and Jon-owland go by themselves? Why should we leave our home?"

I was still gathering my answer when he burst out, "Why don't the strangers just go back across the Big Salt Water?"

"They say the king would harm them if they returned," I told him. "So they stay here and trade with the Abenaki to satisfy their king."

"Have you been to the Abenaki before?"

"Papa has been there with Jon-owland to speak Abenaki," I answered. "But I have not. All of us Wampanoag women prepare the quahog shells to trade."

Mosk had seen me at work gathering, washing, and carving the quahog. The streaks of purple were a bright contrast to the white background. He knew that we traded strings of qua-hog shells for furs. The Abenaki wanted twelve purple quahog shells or twenty of the white shells for each beaver pelt.

"The Strangers call quahog 'wampum' and trade them to other clans," I said, and met his next question before he could ask: "Esapett and Jon-owland want us to live there for a circle of seasons."

"Live there?" Mosk's young voice hit a shrill pitch. "Why would we live in an Abenaki village? Do they like us? Would they want us living among them?"

I tried to think of a simple answer to his question. Though we had long been allies with them against the Narragansett, they were a different clan.

NEXT EVENING, Mama told Mosk to come with her and she told me to accompany them. Mama stepped carefully around the stumps, sharpened by beavers' teeth. It was still light enough to see. Nippa'uus hung gleaming low in the west.

"Look carefully, Mosk, and listen," she said, holding tight to my son's hand.

Standing tall for a boy who'd lived eight circles of seasons, Mosk stopped, first touching the teeth marks in the stump and then looking at the trampled path in the mud leading to where the trees had been dragged to the beaver dam. He squatted down by a hollow log.

"Here's our beaver trap, I helped Papa gather all the por-cupine quills." He put his hand just inside the trap. "We put the quills pointing in so the beaver can go in and find the bait, but can't get back out."

"Ahhe, the quills trap the beaver inside the log," Mama said. "It is a good-spirit trap our people make."

Mosk then pointed to a hard-stone trap closer to the creek. He started toward it. I gasped to see his small hand so close to the dangerous jaws of the trap. "Don't worry," he assured me. "This trap's not set, so we won't get hurt."

"Bad-spirit traps," Mama's quiet voice held a warning. "Can harm you, little grandson, but the worst harm is to our beaver brothers and sisters. These traps the Cloth-men give us take no work to set up, but they kill too many." She looked back up the path we had come on. "The Strangers give us these traps, then they take all the beaver we catch." Mama touched Mosk's arm gently. "Now listen."

Mosk stopped and cocked his head. I stopped too, reaching back to shift Nipi sleeping in her cradleboard on my back. Nipi's breath was so soft that I would not have heard it if there had been any other sound. Mama seemed to be holding her breath. Even the creek was still—no wind, no rocks to make a ripple.

Mama clapped her hands once, the sound reverberating in the silent woods. We waited, a resounding smack came.

Mosk laughed. "Brother Beaver!'

"Or sister," Mama replied. "But only two or three of them are left at their lodge."

We could see the beaver lodge above the dam created by its inhabitants.

"Where is the rest of their family?" my son asked. "When did the Strangers bring iron traps?"

"Sit down here," I told Mosk. I took Nipi's cradleboard from my back, leaning it against a tree. Once unlaced, Nipi joined Mosk and Mama on soft leaves, legs crossed beneath them.

"It started before you were born, Mosk," I said. "It started before I was born, too."

"Ahhe," Mama said, "It even started before I was born, when my own grandmother was a baby and the Wauta-conuag—the Cloth-men—first came across Big Salt Water to Turtle Island."

Mosk leaned against her, twirling a leaf, waiting for the story to unfold. Mama looked at me, her eyes directing me to continue the story.

"The Wauta-conuag wanted the beaver pelts to take back across the Big Salt Water," I said.

"Were these Strangers Esapett and Jon-owland's grandparents' grandparents?" Mosk asked. When I nodded, he continued, "Why do they want to take the pelts back? Why don't they use them for themselves like we do?"

"We don't know," Mama said. "They told us stories we don't understand, with words like 'debt' which they say is a gift that is not really a gift. The giver wants something back."

Mosk looked at me. "Do Strangers use these traps for our beaver?"

"They do not trap, they do not know the ways of beaver. They do not walk much in the land except to use their firesticks to hunt deer and birds. They ask for beaver pelts that we trap. They give us gifts we want—not just the traps, but hardstone tools like axes, hatchet, needles, soft cloth and stout thread. But they don't give us the gifts unless we give them the pelts from our traps."

A little crease formed between Mosk's eyes. "Even our friends?"

"Ahhe, even our friends. If Jon-owland doesn't give enough beaver and other pelts to their people across the Big Salt Water, their sachem—king—won't let them live here."

"But why do we care?" Mosk looked to where his friend's house stood. "If they go back where they come from, we could live here without needing more beaver, and not go to the Abenaki."

My heart wanted to tell Mosk that he was right, if there were no Strangers, our lives could go back to the peace of Grandmother's grandmother's time. But we could not go back to before the Cloth-men brought their bad spirits that killed most of our Wampanoag people, and our enemy Narragansett took over our land. "Our lives are mixed with the Strangers' lives now." I laced Nipi into her cradleboard. "Since Esapett and Jon-owland's people came, they keep the Narragansett away."

Mosk looked around, his eyes following the clouds, the birds, and the splash of a fish on the Big Salt Water. A smile lit his face. "Mama, I know a way we can stay here even if the Strangers go back to their home where Nippa'uus rises. We will make friends with the Narragansett too!"

His words stopped me. "Mosk, the Narragansett want to destroy us! They kidnapped me!" Mosk heard the quiver in my voice and he put a hand on my shoulder. I pulled Mosk into my arms and cradled his head as I'd done when he was a little baby. We rocked silently. Nipi started to wail. I turned to her, but Mama had already gathered her and brought her to me. The four of us embraced.

"What kind of life will our children have?" I whispered to Mama.

Mosk and Nipi stood up and he took her hand as we started for home.

"That's the same question I ask myself," Mama answered. Mama never displayed fear, but our future was fearful.

AFTER THE GRANDMOTHERS' Caucus met, I sat with Mama to do our hair.

"A few of the grandmothers thought that if we give the Strangers no more pelts, they would have to go home, and I agreed," Mama said. "But I told my sister grandmothers that if our friends have to leave, new Cloth-men would come and take their place. We know the new Cloth-men would refuse to be our friends. They would take all our land, our food, even take us."

The Grandmothers' Caucus had talked and thought for several days and nights before reluctantly telling our Massasowet he could negotiate to trade more wampum to the Strangers to buy more Abenaki pelts. "If you and your family live with the Abenaki, you can watch out for Cloth-men demanding too many furs," Mama said as she undid my long braids.

"But I need you to think, Attitash. How will you keep yourself true to our people? Have you become too attached to Esapett?"

I could not answer Mama quickly. There was truth in her words. So I asked, "Do some of the grandmothers think you are also attached to her, or that Papa has become too attached to Jon-owland?"

"Some do." Mama stroked my hair with bear grease and ran her fingers through it. "When the Grandmothers' Caucus learned you might want to go with Esapett up north, they asked if I had approved your joining Esapett so far from our home. One asked why you'd go with the Cloth-woman, saying, 'and Attitash will be with people who do not follow our ways; she already knows their words.'" Mama continued brushing. "I reminded the Grandmothers' Caucus that Esapett came with me to our Moon Lodge so I could cure the sickness in her heart. They understand that I feel closer to Esapett than to the other Strangers. And she has done much to help our family."

I tied strings around the ends of my braids. "Do I need to tell the grandmothers why I must go up north?" I asked.

"The Grandmothers' Caucus does not need you to explain." Mama bent her head so I could reach under the hair that covered her neck and shoulders. "The Grandmothers' Caucus decided you and Black Whale can be trusted to do what's best for the children for seven generations. We will not tell you to go or not to go." As I finished her braids, Mama lifted her head. "You have children, Attitash. We trust you to think of your children, and their children, and their children's children's children."

Elisabeth:

"Has Black Whale or Attitash told you if they'll come with us to Maine?" John asked as we settled down after supper. "It provokes me that they take so long. We need to organize and it makes a difference whether they'll be with us on the boat."

"Not yet. It's a big decision." It had been for me and I would be accompanying my husband. "They have much to consider, and Attitash mentioned talking to her grandmothers."

"Why must they talk to the old women?" John asked as he brought out a trunk full of papers. He'd asked the question ever since he learned of the grandmothers' council. None of my previous attempts to answer made sense to him, so I made no reply.

We took advantage of the quiet and the late summer light to sort through which things to take with us to Maine, which to leave behind, and which to burn. As I went through the few letters my brothers had written, John was looking over his own papers. "Look at this." He held up a letter, written in his bold hand—a copy John had made as clerk for Governor Bradford.

When he handed me the letter, I recalled the stir of pride I'd felt years ago when my reading progressed from stumbling over a few words in the Bible to where John finally trusted me to review his writing. I read aloud the letter's heading. *To Master John Beauchamp, 1626.* He had saved his copy of Bradford's letter for six years.

"Do ye remember when we borrowed one hundred pounds sterling from this Beauchamp in London to pay off the original financiers?" John asked.

I nodded, but truth be told, when he'd shown me the letter six years ago, I was nineteen—a wife and mother, but still too young to understand the meaning within the thicket of words.

"We still have not yet repaid all we borrowed from Beauchamp," John reminded me. "This is why we must move heaven and earth—or at least ourselves—to gain more beaver and timber."

This debt had been like a stone hanging on our necks for

years, our entire life in Plimoth. Before I even had any children.

Looking to check on our children in the garden, the sight of them assured me that we would continue to thrive. Desire had enlisted Hope's help sanding the pots. Little Elizabeth tottered about under her sister Desire's eye, playing with the sand but being kept out of the muck heap and garden beds. Young John was stacking wood. All was well.

I turned back to the letter. It listed my John along with John Alden, William Bradford, Myles Standish, Edward Winslow and William Brewster as 'undertakers' of the debt. Being in such high company would have seemed impossible when we first arrived. Now I was accustomed to my husband's status. I read slowly, trying to comprehend: *And whereas diverse of us have acquainted our worthy and approved friends with our raw and weak estate.* Could John Beauchamp, or any other money lender in London imagine what those words, 'raw and weak,' meant to us? Governor Bradford was no doubt referring to our actual estate—rich in land but lacking any pounds sterling. To me, *raw* meant the vast, heavy woods surrounding us to the west and the endless, heaving sea to the east—forces that compressed my body

Another passage caught my eye: *If therefore God shall move the hearts of any of our friends, in compassion of our wants and present straits, to lend us above named sum.* God had indeed moved John Beauchamp to believe that we would work diligently to pay our debt, despite our raw and weak estate. God desired that we would thrive and multiply in His promised land. Our children would be well and live to have their own children.

I went back to the list of debt undertakers. I had skipped one name and now it singed my tongue when I whispered it, "Isaac Allerton."

John looked up at me. "Thank God Isaac is gone from Plimoth now."

"Has anyone heard from the traitor?" A knock on the door

interrupted John's reply. I opened it a crack and was surprised to see Goody Billington outside.

"Can you spare a moment, Mistress?" She held an empty beaker in one hand and a cloth covered bowl in the other. Goody looked over my shoulder and seeing John stepped back. "Do you mind coming out, Mistress?"

Goody and I sat down on the bench by the door and she handed me the bowl. "I thought you might want some blueberries to make a compote for your journey."

My tongue twisted between speaking my gratitude and asking her what she wanted in return. Taking the bowl, I resisted the question and drew off the cloth. A crow hopped down from the tree and began prancing about. I put the cloth back over the berries, admonishing the crow to keep her distance. "These look like fine berries, Goody. Did ye pick them?"

Goodwife Billington shrugged, "I had help." She watched the crow fly back to the tree.

"We had crows back home in England."

I lifted the cover again and fingered the berries. Maybe they were gratitude for when John and I'd helped Goody and her son Francis clear out her husband's effects two years ago. A rather long time to show gratitude, but still a nice gesture. "This was most kind of you."

"'Twas nay trouble." Goody picked up the empty beaker. Her face was impassive.

The crow cawed loudly. A responding caw came from beyond the fence.

Goody looked out to the receding tide and calm sea. "You may have crows and berries up north, too."

"I expect we might." I gave her my first smile. "And God will be there too."

With a flap of wings and loud cawing, the crow flew towards the answering call.

"Crows will steal anything." Goody watched the crow

disappear, then turned to me. "I was sore afraid when my husband was hanged for murdering John Newcomen. Thought I'd be hanged, too." She clenched her fists.

"Why did ye think so? Ye killed no one." I was moved to take her hand, but didn't. Pride kept her hands fisted. Since John Billington was hanged, Goody's eye had not been blackened nor her cheeks bruised and swollen. But healing in the heart takes longer.

"Mistress, you know how blame flies around our plantation like a swarm of mosquitoes."

"Yea, Goody. We both know that, don't we?"

Was she apologizing for when she'd joined those accusing me of witchcraft? That was nigh unto ten years ago. The curse would never release its hold on me!

"Mistress, I thought the savage's medicine was witchcraft, but Mistress Brewster told me that it works and I should ask you or your friend for…." Goodwife Billington blinked her eyes fast, fighting a stray tear. "My husband was still alive then and she urged me to get something to heal my husband's…his hand print." Goody put her hands over her cheeks and drew a deep breath. "I didn't dare ask you for help after what I'd said about thy heathen friend."

I'd been cleansed of my anger toward those who accused me, but now my heart eased even more. I looked at the beaker. "What do ye need medicine for now?"

"Night sweats. Mistress Hopkins told me the heathen gave you something."

Attitash and I had learned how lethal a large dose could be. A small dose of black cohosh did help soothe the change-of-life symptoms like night sweats. "I have some of the roots in store. I'll have to pound them and give thee a decoction tomorrow."

Goody handed me the beaker and bowed slightly, as if I were royalty.

"Can ye get through another night, Goodwife?"

"Thank you kindly. I've gotten through all the others."

I shut the door behind Goodwife Billington. John waited for an explanation, but I simply said, "Goody gave us berries."

"Stay," John said. "Goody Billington would never come just to give thee berries. Might she still be seeking thy punishment for witchcraft?"

I wondered if my husband—or I for that matter—would ever feel free of the accusations I endured as a girl. "Trust me, Dear Heart," I assured him. "I am careful of what the goodwife asks. But in this instance she was seeking a remedy for womanly troubles."

John looked at me with a wry smile. "And thus do our womenfolk disguise their suspicions. Mayhap she looks to see if ye attempt to give her some of Satan's brew."

"It is ever thus that our faithful husbands do seek to find their suspicions justified," I replied. "Goody wished me well on our journey and gave me the berries in exchange. Now may I return to the subject at hand?"

I picked up a copy of Bradford's 1626 letter to Beauchamp again and read a passage describing how Isaac Allerton, who, as treasurer of our colony, would be delivering the payment on Beauchamp's loan.

"If only our leaders had known then how despicable Allerton is." I put down the letter, too disturbed to read. "It tore my soul when he was trusted with our finances."

"If anyone had asked thee, ye would have told them not to trust Allerton," John replied.

"No one would listen to me!" The terror of facing Allerton's accusations still warped my heart. "Remember, Elder Brewster trusted Allerton to read scripture to us at services, though he obviously paid no attention to the admonitions to be good and faithful servants!"

"To read the truth is not to live the truth," John agreed.

"There was too much bad blood between Allerton and me. I'd thought I was his only prey when I was fourteen and

Allerton assassinated my character in his attempt to indenture me to his household. In fact, we were all his prey." I read the passage again. "This letter was written after Allerton married Fear Brewster, our dear Elder and Mistress's daughter." I shoved down the vile taste that filled my mouth when I thought of Fear Brewster marrying the twisted-hearted Isaac Allerton. "Mistress had admitted to me privately that she carried reservations," I continued ruefully. "I'd attempted to put aside my own feelings and assured her. 'Many say that all Master Allerton needs is a mother for his children.'"

"Yea, but Elder and Mistress Brewster gave their approval of their own free will," John assured me. "Who knew that when Allerton delivered the profits for timber and pelt to the financiers, the snake stole some for himself each time."

"But how did he practice the deceit? Why did no one know the bloody man stole from his own people?" At the time all this transpired I'd been mired in my own personal trauma associated with Allerton and had not paid attention to his financial shenanigans.

"Do ye not remember that Isaac altered our plantation's financial records? All we knew was that the debt hardly decreased." John passed his hand over his eyes as if relieving his memory.

"I'd not noticed the details," I answered somewhat defensively. John knew the vile Allerton had vilified me when I weaseled out of his effort to take me as an indentured servant.

"Isaac Allerton's soul was lost to greed. Any ill-gotten gains Allerton kept for himself." John put his arm around me. "And that greed included possessing thee, Dear Heart."

"It did," I leaned into him. "So tell me again, since I was not involved in our colony's finances, how did we discover the theft?"

"Do ye recall that Beauchamp and our leaders reviewed the loan terms in 1628 and discovered Allerton's failure to pay Beauchamp in full from our revenue? That's when the knave was banished from Plimoth, and we could finally pay down the debt without lining Allerton's pocket."

The letter and our conversation finally made clear to me what had been a heart-wrenching and confusing disaster. "But Fear Brewster, his poor wife, and the children still carry the shame of his betrayal." My voice choked.

I handed John a parcel of my brother's letters and he packed them with his own to save for our return from Maine. "I still carry anger, John. I pray I will be able to forgive him. Have ye forgiven him?"

"I am praying, too." John rubbed his hands through his dark hair. "If ye pray for thy own ability to forgive, pray for mine too." John closed the lid on the letter box and turned to pack his ammunition bandoliers. "It's between God and Allerton now."

John's admission that he felt as I did eased me. Needing respite, I picked up my shawl. "There's a little time before dark. I want to go visit Burial Hill."

John looked up in surprise. "We don't leave for Maine for two weeks yet. I thought we'd go together later to say farewell to all our loved ones."

"Of course." I glanced out at the children, still playing in our garden. "But I want to see Mistress Brewster's grave tonight."

I KNELT DOWN AND TOUCHED the small marker with my fingers. Would she know what her son-in-law had done to her family? The wind coming off the sea swished my skirts. I pulled them tight and leaned close to Mistress Brewster's grave. "We will let God deal with Isaac Allerton," I whispered. "Fear and her sister Patience are strong women. I will keep my promise to be their good-sister."

The sun was streaking the western hills. I was loathe to leave my dear ones' graves. If we returned safely from Maine, it would still be at least a year before I could come to the burial ground again. But I needed to bed down my children. As I walked down the hill, I could see figures coming to my house. The twilight obscured them until I was closer. Attitash! Did she bring good news or bad on their coming with us to Maine?

The stillness in her face as I approached told me that she carried a strong opinion. But I did not understand what it was until she embraced me with the words, "We will go with you."

"I must leave my family, my parents, all my people, and bring my children to strange land," Attitash said as we drew apart.

Searching her face, I realized that I had no means to reward her for the sacrifice. "Catabatash, netop," I thanked my friend, in her words.

"My John will be glad if Black Whale can drive one of our oxen," I told Attitash. "Would ye come with us on the shallop or walk with him?"

Attitash drew a deep breath, as she always did when she needed to ponder the best decision. "Neither one seems an easy way," she answered, "As it is with most choices I must make to help your people."

Her small smile as she touched my cheek assured me that she was willing to choose between the lesser of two evils. Truth be told, I did not myself relish the thought of traveling along the rocky coast in a small bouncing shallop, nor the long walk through hostile territory.

3

1632
WAMPANOAG TERRITORY
CAPE COD BAY

Attitash:

My father tried to assure me it would be safer to go on the wind canoe than to walk with Black Whale. "The trail to Abenaki country is dangerous. You will be with Jonowland and his men as they ride the small wind-canoe on Big Salt Water," Papa said. I'd watched the small wind-canoe every time Papa went trading on it with the Strangers. Their wind-canoes sit too high, bouncing on the water. Our own dug-out canoes sit low in the water, like fish-eating birds. I thought Papa was only reassuring me with tales.

"It could be dangerous for a woman carrying a pack through the Massachuseuk's land, Papa said. "The Cloth-men they call, 'Weston's rabble,' nearly destroyed the Massachuseuk land and their families," Papa continued. "They blame us and our friendship with our Strangers for not warring against Thomas Weston, the Stranger they saw as our friend. If he'd been killed or driven back, the evil Cloth-men would not have preyed upon the Massachuseuk in their home."

"Don't they know?" I asked, "We helped our Strangers fight the Weston rabble and win. Cap-an Standish even brought back one of their foul heads and put it on their fence."

Papa smiled. "And I was there to enjoy the sight." He continued sharpening his arrows with his stone. "But the Weston rabble still remain in Massachuseuk lands."

Mama agreed with Papa that I should go by water. They had already agreed with Black Whale that my brother, Fish Hawk, should accompany him on the trail. However, Mama had her own opinion on why to go by sea instead of land, which she explained as we walked to the hill that looked down on the shore.

"Black Whale does not need your help on the trail. He is taking one of great-beasts, that the Strangers call ox, to carry all the packs." She laced her fingers in mine. "And you know the new ox-beasts have very sharp hooves and could kick you or Mosk, step on your feet or even bite."

I shared my mother's fear, though my husband and son did not. "There seems to be danger both ways," I told her. The silver streaks in Mama's hair sparkled from the light coming over the hills to the west.

After we walked back to our home, I blew on an ember in the fire until it flamed to life. "When we get to the Kennebec River, we will keep a children's fire with the Abenaki. They also build a small fire to remind everyone that decisions must look ahead to seven generations of our children's children."

"I wish our children's children would not have to depend on the Cloth-men," Mama murmured. "But there are too many of them. We have to drink from their water jar as well as our own."

That night I dreamt.

The sky-fire gods poured fire and water down. I huddled in a whale canoe; Mosk hung onto my braids. Heaving water swept us out and closed over our heads, pulling us down in the water. Bubbles rose above me as I struggled for breath. Then an ox-beast bumped me gently and swam under me. She rose, her back carrying me. When she swam out from under us, I grabbed with all my strength and found her tailbone, beneath the hair of its tail. The ox-beast pulled us up, up, up—Mosk still clinging to my braids. My chest was a stone. We all surfaced, I gulped air, let go, and landed on the sand.

I woke shivering from my dream. It filled my heart and I knew I could not go in the small wind-canoe with Esapett.

As the dream faded, I wondered if the ox-beasts really could swim. Were these creatures my friends or enemies? I pushed the dream away and pulled my son close to me. I would not go on the sea and be drowned, but what would it be like walking the trails with this beast? Black Whale assured me that he would prefer his own feet and would only use the ox-beast to carry packs. It seemed that walking a trail, with no one riding on the beast, carried less danger than a stormy sea. Sitting up, I took big breaths to blow away the shreds of fear from the dream.

Aunt Blue Sky was awake too, pouring herself a cup of water. I greeted her quietly.

"Attitash, have you decided how to travel?" Aunt Blue Sky asked.

"I think so." I sat down beside the fire with her. "Black Whale is taking an ox-beast on the journey. I'm not sure if walking with it will be easier or more dangerous."

"Maybe you'll sit on one and rest." She laughed as she squatted on a log, pretending to be on the big animal.

"Have you sat on them?" I asked my aunt. We had all learned to sit on the great-heads—the ones we learned to call "horse." These "oxen" were too broad to sit on!

Aunt Blue Sky laughed again. "I think my bones are too old to learn a new way to sit." I smiled, glad I no longer felt her presence an intrusion.

Many new-green-leaf-seasons ago, Aunt Blue Sky, Mama's Otter Clan sister, came to live with my family after her husband was killed by the Sky Fire God. Mama had told me that Aunt Blue Sky was becoming a sister-wife. I assumed that meant Aunt Blue Sky would live in our wetu. I loved my Otter Clan aunt. She helped Grandmother teach me the ways of women before my first life-flow. I was glad to have her. Mama, Grandmother, and I gave Aunt Blue Sky much comfort with healing ceremonies for several moons.

When the cold moons had come and gone, Grandmother gave Aunt Blue Sky a cleansing ceremony. The full meaning of her presence became clear that night when Papa joined Aunt Blue Sky in her place on the sleeping benches, while Mama slept alone. I pulled my deerskin over my head and snuggled in close to Black Whale, so I would not be faced with the obvious. When I woke in the dark later, I heard the small sounds of mating. I crammed my hand into my mouth, but still my voice pushed past my hand with a soft cry of protest. Black Whale's warmth surrounded me, but I felt cold. I did not want to imagine a second wife taking Black Whale to her bed.

After waking, I could not talk to Mama or Aunt Blue Sky. They seemed content as they went about building up the fire and stirring the pots. Mama called me to her later that morning while she was pounding deerskins. Although I was long a grown woman, Mama still noticed when I pulled my feelings inside my head and did not talk to her. She nearly always knew why and did not ask now what troubled me. I wondered if her own father had taken a sister-wife in addition to Grandmother.

"Did you not learn anything when training for your first moon lodge?" Mama kept her eyes on her work. She knew I would listen. "What did the Grandmothers tell you about our People needing many babies to strengthen our numbers?"

I sat down by my mother and looked back at the voices and pictures in my head. "They taught us that Our People needed to always consider what is needed for children in seven generations. We must bring more new life to keep our Wampanoag nation strong."

"Ahhe, so you do remember. And did they remind you that with all the deaths brought by Strangers' Bad Spirits, and so many of our men killed by Strangers, we Wampanoag are small in number?" When I nodded, she continued, "If Esapett's people had not come to our shores with their bad spirits when my grandmother's grandmother was alive, our people would still be strong. We would not have so few men. We would not be desperate to bring so many babies into the world."

I knew Mama spoke the truth. The Strangers had so many men and so few women. We had so few men, but we had many good ones to their few like Jon-owland. It was not Esapett's fault, but it was her people's fault. "I do know this, Mama."

Mama touched my hand lightly. "Then you know why the grandmothers taught you that women must share a husband so that more babies will be born."

I shifted my hips so the strange ache in my woman-place would ease. "That all seemed natural to me as a young girl. I had not fallen in love with Black Whale then."

Mama smiled, but it was not a taunting smile. "Ahhe, so do you believe that only sharing love can make the seed grow?" She waited while I picked at the leavings of brittle leather she was scraping off the hide.

"Does Aunt Blue Sky want to mate with Papa?"

Mama gave me a straight-line mouth. "She thinks of her own husband, of Seekonk, who is now in the spirit world."

I remembered Aunt Blue Sky and Uncle Seekonk together, their delight in their love. She had comforted Uncle Seekonk after he lost his first family at Patuxet when the Strangers' bad spirits took them.

"What did you just tell me we all need to do, Attitash? "

"Think of our people in seven generations." I knew what Mama wanted to hear and kept my eyes down to speak, "And we must have enough babies so our people will continue."

I remembered that Papa had returned to Mama's bed once Aunt Blue Sky's belly showed. Her Otter clan son, Little Moose, was born in the next cold moon. He now stood as tall as my own son.

Aunt Blue Sky poured hot water from the kettle into a birch bark pan and sprinkled corn into it, then raised her eyes to mine. "I will miss you and your family, Attitash. Come home safe."

Wᴇ sᴛᴀʀᴛᴇᴅ ᴏᴜʀ journey on foot the next day. Having embraced Mama, Aunt Blue Sky, and my sister, White Flower, I did not look back. My son kept waving goodbye to his grandparents, long after we'd started on the trail. I could not let Mosk see me sad at leaving my family. He was so young, he probably expected to see them again in a circle of Nippa'uus.

Black Whale walked first. Mosk ran between his father and me. Following me, my brother, Little Fish, led the ox, loaded with our supplies. I was glad I did not have to walk behind the beast, who plopped dung onto the trail.

Despite my apprehension, our journey was quiet the first few circles of Nippa'uus. Mosk danced about the trail the first morning as if he were one of the small forest spirits. When our son got tired and wanted to rest, Black Whale boosted him up on the ox-beast. I protested, my breath catching with worry, but Mosk squealed with delight as the beast snorted, then stamped his front feet. As it began lowering its head, Little Fish pulled the ox-beast up with the taut rope.

My brother laughed when I demanded my son walk instead. "As his Clan Uncle, I will keep him safe," he assured me. He led the ox a few steps and it settled down.

"Just don't turn around and look at them," Black Whale said, laughing at my fears.

From time to time, our trail would allow us a view of the Big Salt Water. It was quiet, the water birds bobbed up and down, watching for food without fear of rough waves. When we camped for the night, I prayed to the Sky Spirits for clear skies. Mosk was quickly asleep. I wondered how Esapett and Pah-scilla got their babes to sleep on the crowded wind-canoe. Both carried new life, which they would deliver in the North Country if the wind-canoe did not cause them to deliver too early. Mosk was so dear to me. And I still held the memory of my first child, who left me for the Spirit World before she saw the light. It was fear for my living child that kept me away from the wind-canoe crowded with Strangers.

On clear nights, Black Whale checked the stars to see where we were. He informed me one evening that we were close to where the bad Weston Strangers had lived in Massachuseuk territory. "There should be no one here now," he assured me. "It is many circles of seasons since our friends sent most of them back across the Big Salt Water." I said nothing but kept my eyes open. I knew some of these bad Cloth-men had gone to other settlements.

Early one morning, we stopped at a spring to fill our water jugs. Mosk was tossing stones into the little water ripples when he froze. I followed his eyes above the water and saw a glimmer of hair. The hair disappeared into the thicket surrounding the spring. I pulled Mosk to me and whistled to Black Whale. He and Little Fish were adjusting the packs on the beast but turned at my whistle.

Eyes, nearly covered by lank hair, stared out at me from the thicket. Then the full face looked out and her mouth moved. The sound was so raspy I could not be sure I heard, but it sounded like, "Attitash."

Seafoam was in those eyes.

I cried out her name as Black Whale came back to us. She slowly stood up and crept out of the thicket. Her bones seemed to poke through what little flesh she carried. Her dress and poncho were torn and filthy. She staggered toward us as I broke through bushes to catch her. Pushing her hair back, I saw scars on her face. When we were becoming women, Seafoam's pretty face was a barrier to our cousin-sister closeness. My childish fear, that she would be more desirable than I, pulled my heart away from her. Now, safe in my husband's love, I could only despair the harm done to Seafoam. The glow of promise so evident in her youth was dimmed, not only by the streaks of rigid skin revealing burns, but by harm to her spirit.

"Seafoam," I whispered, "You're safe with me." Pulling journey cake from my belt, I fed her bits and gave her water. But we had to keep going, it was a long walk to the Abenaki in Maine. We had to get there before the big snows came.

Elisabeth:

My husband was occupied with directing the men to the multitude of tasks involved in sailing. It was up to us women to prevent our children from falling overboard, and even when they were safe aboard, we had to keep the little ones out of the men's way. Priscilla and I put the older girls in charge of the toddling babes. I was tending to my youngest when I caught sight of my young John leaning over the rail. I hollered at him, but to no avail over the wind wailing, waves crashing, gulls shrieking and men shouting. As I tried to make my way over, a young man grabbed my boy and pulled him back from the rail.

"This be yours, Mistress?" he asked, his eyes crinkling in laughter at my son's attempt to stand tall and look older. I reached for young John, but Moses Talbot kept his hand on the boy's shoulder. "His father has too much to look after." Talbot glanced at my daughter, Desire, holding her little sister, Hope. My baby Elizabeth clutched my neck and the bulge under my skirt showed.

"Begging your pardon, so do you also, Mistress."

"I do what?" I inquired. Moses Talbot was probably close to my age, about 25, but unencumbered by family. Did he know what it took to keep track of a young boy aboard a small shallop?

"By your leave, the boy can help me with these ropes."

I nodded as Talbot took the boy in hand, showing him how to watch the curl of slack ropes so it would not trip him as the wind caught the sails and the ropes tightened. Evidently, Talbot knew how to handle a young boy.

For the rest of the morning, I kept my eye on the pair, often close enough that I could hear the narrative Moses gave of our voyage. His light blue eyes glinted as he described the curve of Cape Cod and how we would follow this curve, staying out of the big waves of the Atlantic. As Talbot turned to me from time to time, his golden hair escaping from the restraining thong and blowing across his face, he informed me of the progress of our journey.

When John finally found time to join me for our light meal of cheese, dried fish and biscuits, he nodded with distracted assent when I explained the help Talbot provided.

"He's a good young man—strong."

I had noticed myself that Moses Talbot had shoulders as broad as my husband's and the muscles in his arms pushed against his shirt. My John was now forty years old, and if anything, even stronger than when we first met. But there is a certain vigor to youth.

"Just so he does not neglect his duties." John swallowed a mouthful of cheese, then catching my look, grinned. "Nay, wife. I don't think watching son John is not important, too; but each man must do his job or the ship won't carry us north. I'll warn little John to mind his mother and not bother Talbot when he's busy."

Attitash:
Seafoam struggled to keep up with us. One leg did not want to hold her weight, but she refused to ride on the great-beast

or allow me to carry her. She did let me keep her small pack and took my hand when the trail was too bumpy. Still, she delayed us. Our plan had been to hurry through the Massachuseuk territory where the Weston Strangers lived. Now, we were easy prey for anyone wishing to attack us.

Finally, Black Whale insisted. "Get on my back for now."

"Mata!" Seafoam curled into a ball.

"You either get on my back or on Little Fish's or on the great-beast. This pace will lead us straight into enemy hands."

Seafoam peeked between her arms. The whites of her eyes flashed. I could see her fear of my husband and brother was as great as of the beast. "I can carry you a little way," I told her. I gave Nipi's cradleboard and the packs to my brother to carry as he led the great-beast, which caused more delay as the beast adjusted to the additions.

Seafoam uncurled and I leaned down so she could rest on my back. We did go slowly, but not as slow as before.

We made it safely to a place we could camp by dark. I heated water to wash her thoroughly. Her bad leg had bruises where she'd fallen, but my heart squeezed with pain when I saw that Seafoam's breasts and belly showed welts, the kind made by someone using a switch.

Finally, like unweaving a basket, Seafoam told her story.

Her Narragansett husband had abandoned her, trading her to one of the bad Weston Strangers for a mere firestick. The Weston stranger brought her back to a hovel that could not be called a home. She would not speak of his abuse, but her suffering showed on her body and in her eyes. Fear sparked in them whenever Black Whale spoke. His deep voice was a comfort to me, but the tight hunch in Seafoam's shoulders betrayed a wariness deep in her body.

"Long after Esapett's men came and fought the Massachuseuk, the evil man and his pack began preparing to sail back across the Big Salt Water," Seafoam said in a weary voice. "I escaped and fled. For two moons I've survived by myself. Afraid to go near the Massachuseuk, I ran whenever I thought anyone was nearby."

She stopped talking, tremors rippling in her face. "I heard the great-beast's low cry and hid before it could smell my fear. The brush was so thick and I was so tired that I could not out-run anything. Then I peeked out and nearly fainted with relief to see you." Seafoam gripped her elbows, hugging herself. "You found me, dear sister-cousin."

I gently took her hands. She wept. I wept. Mosk hid behind his papa.

That night I slept between Black Whale and Seafoam, Mosk curled with Little Fish on the other side of his papa. If I had not been so weary, I might have considered how this sleeping arrangement might ripple into our new life up north.

Elisabeth:

As our shallop moved north toward Maine, I tried to recognize the coastline from our map. Cape Cod curled in a great circle and Massachuseuk territory was close to Plimoth. However, from the sea it all looked the same—water, sand, trees, with the sun going down over the green hills and coming up next morning over the water. Morning fog obscured our passage most days. We delayed sailing until it cleared.

Late afternoon, we sailed close to shore and caught the change in the air coming from small settlements. The green smell faded and a heavier odor floated across the river that crept with the tide from the sea into a harbor. I stood drinking in the sights of gulls screaming and diving.

"Mama," my son pointed to shore, "Moses says that's Boston."

"Goodman Talbot, to you, not Moses." I slapped little John's wrist lightly so he'd learn his manners. I beckoned to Talbot. "Don't let him get fresh with you."

Moses Talbot cuffed the boy. "Listen to thy mother."

"Aye, Sir." Young John managed to look chastised though he obviously felt nothing. "But tell my mother about Boston, where the King's men are trying to steal the timber and beaver away from us."

"I'm sure thy father has informed her. He knows much more than I."

A shout alerted us all to a longboat, coming toward us from shore.

"The Bostonians," my John called out. He waved an arm at the boat but kept the shallop moving north with no attempt to exchange words with the small boat. It turned back to shore and quickly disappeared between the waves.

That night when we finally were bedded down with all the others, I snuggled close to my husband and whispered, "Who are the men in Boston trying to take away our timber and trapping rights?"

John sighed the deep breath of a man desperate for sleep. "I don't know their names. The Boston settlers think they have the rights to everything north. The Bostonians claim that Koussinoc –the Abenaki trading post—should be theirs and they want our trading rights." He settled his arms around me. "That's why we are going to take charge of the trading post, as I told thee."

"I remember what ye told me, but now I wonder if the Boston lot will try to intercept our little shallop."

"Not to worry," John stroked my cheek. "We have the King's patent and our presence at Koussinoc will remind any poachers there are now armed men to enforce it." My husband's arms enfolded me. "Go to sleep now, Dear Heart."

Sleep did not come quickly, but I finally succumbed to dreams.

Attitash:

One night's rest did not restore Seafoam's leg. She tried to stand but lost her balance and I had to catch her.

"You can't walk." I shifted Nipi's cradleboard to ease my shoulders. "And I can't hold you and carry the cradleboard."

Seafoam did not answer. Her eyes stayed on the ground.

"Mosk has taken rides on the great-beast," I continued. "You must be as brave as my little son, Seafoam."

Black Whale looked up at Nippa'uus, already climbing the blue sky. "There's no other way to keep moving."

Seafoam's mouth quivered and she put her hands over her eyes. "I'm too much burden. Just leave me here."

I took hold of her shoulders and shook her. "Stop acting like a child. We have many days' walk ahead of us. You will die if you stay here. Ride the great-beast."

Getting Seafoam on the great-beast was like trying to pick up a stubborn goat. Fear of the creature clenched her muscles and she could not get a leg up, even with my hand providing a lift. I had to show her.

Black Whale held the rope taut around the great-beast's thick neck and cupped his hand to hold my foot. He boosted me onto the beast and I folded one leg in front of me and let the other hang. My position felt precarious. The creature felt my tension and tried to back up. Black Whale kept hold of the rope and it stopped but swung its head back at me as if to bite. Its back twitched while I clung desperately to its horn with one hand and grabbed a hank of neck hair with the other. Seafoam's squealing did not help.

"Why is he fighting me?" I asked. "Does he not like women on his back?"

Black Whale lifted an eyebrow and smiled. "He does not want anyone, woman, man or child on his back."

Hanging onto the rope around his neck, I used my knee and thigh for leverage to rise a little off the beast's back. The creature stiffened and tossed its head. Black Whale spoke quietly to the beast, just as he did with our dogs, and astonishingly, the creature quieted.

I tucked my deerskin skirt between my bottom and the great-beast's back. It snorted quietly. Black Whale allowed it to take a few steps. It seemed almost like I was in a longboat, going up and down. We walked a short ways, then Black Whale told Seafoam she had to get on the beast.

"I can't. These beasts work the Clothmen's fields. They don't carry people." Seafoam stood with wide eyes and clenched hands. "It will bite me."

"They won't bite unless they've been mistreated," Black Whale told her, keeping his voice light and reassuring.

"Can it tell when the person trying to ride it has been mistreated?" Seafoam asked. "It will try to stab me with its horns if I get near."

Black Whale gave Seafoam a long-nose look which left no opening for arguing. He made no attempt to soften his deep voice. "You don't have a choice, Seafoam. Get on or I'll put you on!"

Seafoam bit her lip and shifted her bad leg. Black Whale moved to her side and picked Seafoam up, dropping her behind me.

"Sit up. Treat the beast like you would a good dog," he said.

"You are treating me like a bad dog," she hissed at Black Whale. He just laughed.

I turned around so I could look at Seafoam. The whites in her eyes showed, but she grabbed my waist as she bent her injured leg over the beast and the good leg under herself.

"Ox," she patted its rump, trying the Strangers' word for the great-beast.

At first, she clutched me so tightly that my breath was caught. The beast lurched with stiff legs. Black Whale still held the rope or we would have been shaken off.

The song came unbidden from my throat, "Hush a bye, Baby, on the tree top, when the wind blows the cradle will rock." Both the ox and my cousin relaxed.

Now that Seafoam was settled, I slid down. Black Whale could again lead our procession with his bow and arrow in hand. Little Fish brought up the rear, holding the rope for the ox. Seafoam clung to its horns. Young Mosk ran back and forth between us, checking on Seafoam, and then catching up with me to hold my hand.

Elizabeth:

After five days of sailing, large boulders and rocks were visible along the shore. Sometimes the sea dashed against rocks, leaving no place to safely land. When we could not get to shore, we would anchor as close to land as possible.

On the sixth night of our voyage, we slept as always under the sail pulled over our sleeping quarters. Bright moonlight lit up the sail so it glowed above our heads. Everyone else seemed to be sleeping, but not I. John could usually persuade me not to worry, but now we were moving our entire family to an unknown place in a wilderness far from home and help. I tried to take my mind from such matters by counting how many days' worth of biscuits we'd packed. That only increased my tension. My mind slipped to the considerate way Moses Talbot had of explaining things— both to my son and to me.

When John was breathing deeply, I extracted myself from the tangle of sleeping bodies and crawled out. The full moon left a trail that heaved with the waves. I drank in the beauty, feeling my worries fade. A familiar silhouette perched on the mainsail mast. Was it a crow? Were we close enough to the land that a crow could fly out and trespass onto the seagulls' territory? Was this crow a harbinger of good fortune or bad? My unborn babe fluttered in my belly. Would this child come safely in the land so strange to us? I crawled back to our covered sleep quarters and sank into a restless sleep.

The river was swift, full of rapids. Standing on shore, I could see the shallop, moving slowly upstream. Shots rang out. My John called out to me across the water. But I could not make out what he said.

"Talbot, Moses Talbot," I said to John in a whisper, putting my fingers on his mouth to remind him not to wake the others. "I dreamed he was shot."

"What? Who?" John rubbed his eyes and raised his head off the pillow. In the dim moonlight his eyes fixed on me like I was the dream. Everyone around us slept, faint ghosts crowded in slumber in the faint moonlight that filtered through the sail pulled over our heads.

He responded with a slight rasp to his low voice, "Why ever would ye dream that?"

I gave no answer, having none.

"And why Moses Talbot?" John sat up. "Am I not in thy dreams anymore?"

"Ye want me to dream ye are shot, John?"

He chuckled and I realized my vivid dream was just a joke to him. It provoked me so that I pulled the cover up over my face.

Putting my mouth close to his ear, I said quietly, "I don't know anything. But it woke me in a fright."

John pulled me tight against him. "I did see Talbot taking care of our boy. Did he treat him well?"

"Yea, he was very nice to young John."

"Then, ye do not want Talbot done in?"

I smiled and sighed. "No, of course not." I took a long breath and stroked my darling husband's shoulders, comforting myself. He responded by tightening his arms around me.

"So what does it mean?" I asked him.

John kissed my cheek, then slid one hand to cup my breast. "It may mean nothing. Or it may mean…." He stopped, perhaps unwilling to tell me a hard truth about what we faced. "Just sleep now, Love. Soon we'll be in our own little home at Koussinoc—in Maine. Ye will sleep well, just us and our children then. Sweet dreams."

I let my breath out slowly, feeling his warmth seep into my body.

Attitash:

When we stopped that night, the ox looked like a spirit in the round moon's eerie light. I closed my eyes when we wrapped our furs around us in the same sleeping order, feeling my cousin on one side and Black Whale on the other. Not wanting to look at Seafoam's face, I turned my back to her and reached to my husband. My hand slid between his legs, a gesture that usually brought distracting excitement. Now, I was too aware of Seafoam and withdrew my hand.

Black Whale responded by taking my hand and replacing it. I refrained from stroking him but did cup his warm man-sacs. When his sighs threatened to alert Seafoam and our children, I removed my hand. "We must wait," I said.

He gently answered my light caresses. "They'll be asleep soon."

I listened to Seafoam's breathing. It was slowing, but I could not rely on her staying asleep.

Aware that it would diffuse our desire, I asked Black Whale, "Why do the Strangers cut the male great-beasts? Don't they want more baby beasts?"

"Of course, but these oxen can't run wild like all creatures should. The Strangers keep them captive. I know their urge to escape to find mates who accepts them." His arms tightened around me. "Jon-owland says the males get frustrated, trying to mount females that resist." He chuckled.

My woman-place clenched, remembering the Narragansett men trying to take us against our will. It no longer mattered to me whether Seafoam slept. I only wanted Black Whale's arms about me, nothing more.

4

Elisabeth:

As we sailed north of Boston, the shore completely lost any form of beach as rocks and boulders sluiced heavy breakers into rivulets. We woke into another world composed of many changing hues in shifting mists, the sounds of water crashing and fierce wind pushing our little shallop toward the rocks. The men rang the ship's bell continually.

"Mother, we can't see rocks or other boats," my little John informed me with the excitement of a boy who fears nothing, "That's why the bell rings!"

My husband gave the order to sail further out to sea as we all clung to the rail, listening both to our bell and for a possible response.

My children hovered with me, only young John restlessly jumping up to look about. Desire, with all the bossiness of the oldest child, pulled at her brother to sit and be quiet. Their father was too occupied with sailing to listen to his son's attempts to escape being caught by a sister.

Moses Talbot leaned over and took young Desire's hand. "Don't worry about thy brother, Lass."

I was holding Hope and baby Elizabeth and nodded my

thanks for his assistance. Catching my John's eye as he turned to survey the boat, I tried to put on a calm face. Just then a shout came up—a silhouette in the east, emerging from the fog. They hauled the lines, attempting to turn the boat about, away from the dark shape.

"Another boat?" Priscilla asked me. I gave her no answer. The dark shape continued toward us, seemingly heedless of the bell ringing madly. Probably couldn't hear it with all the waves surging and wind blowing, I feared. A bleak streak of sunlight broke through the fog and lit up the shape. No sails in view, only the dark shadow rising above the water. Then it disappeared. I rubbed my eyes.

A shout rose as the shape broke the water, advancing on our little shallop. "It's not a ship at all," I murmured.

"Whale!" The call rose from John Alden. It was not the small black one we call grampus, but a large whale.

"Don't crowd the rails," my John shouted as the shallop listed when we rushed to get a better look. Most of us backed off, and the shallop righted. Nothing stopped the whale's rising and falling in the sea as it pursued us. A vision of its huge head smashing into our boat mingled with fear that the creature might have tentacles with which to reach into our company and snatch a child.

Some men had their muskets out, loading powder, but there was no fire to use for a light. My John and John Alden exhorted the men to put their backs into the oars, though we all knew with such a wind that it was futile.

"Will the whale jump on board?" Desire cried. I pushed all the children down and lay on top of them, hoping somehow to protect them. Who knew if the whale could leap onto the shallop or if it would go underneath us and launch us into the air, smashing the boat and tossing us into the sea?

The wind screamed and the waves smashed against the shallop. We huddled in a heap, with Priscilla and her children next to us.

"Turn-about!" The desperate shout came amidst the cacophony. I thought it was hopeless to attempt fleeing the whale. Our little shallop could never maneuver out of the whale's path. I raised my head, hoping to see the whale losing ground or going back out to sea. I could see nothing but waves crashing and our sail taut in the wind.

"We're doomed," Priscilla shouted over the wind. I wanted to clap my hand over my friend's mouth. Our children were frightened already—no need to further provoke their fears. My mind skittered around the possibilities of survival if the whale dove under our shallop and upended it. Only my little Elizabeth was screaming—and she too young to know the danger. Barely able to walk, she only knew she wanted out from under me.

"Yea, Praise God!" came another cry. "The whale turned."

I raised my head. The men hollered and waved their arms. I grabbed Priscilla's arm and she raised her head too.

"Saved." I said. My voice choked with relief.

ORDER WAS restored on the boat when the fog lifted at last. The whale was not to be seen. We continued north, aiming for a calm place to drop the anchor and batten down for the night. When John returned to my side, we sat wordlessly, our clasped hands the only communication needed.

Later, after a small supper of dried biscuits and peas, the children slept. John and I leaned our heads together for a bit of privacy. We were compelled by the day's events to touch each other everywhere, assuring ourselves we had indeed survived. Reminding each other of our constant love brought tears to my eyes. A couple of sweet kisses and I prepared to sleep when John murmured. "Was Talbot paying attention to our little girl?"

"Desire? Well, he tried to keep her from scolding her brother. Why?"

"He could have plans for her later."

"She's but nine years old. What are ye talking about?" I protested, letting my voice rise above a whisper. "And Talbot must be near my age."

"Yea, Moses is about twenty-three. Fourteen years older than our lass."

It was hard to tell in the dark, but John seemed to be smiling.

"What if we'd met when ye were but a nine-year-old lass?" John's chuckle escaped. "What would thy father have thought?"

I giggled back and dug my elbow into his side. "Do ye think my father approved when we met and I was thirteen? Ye were a twenty-eight-year-old man!"

"I hope thy father knew I did not lust after thee when we first met."

I could hardly bring up my father's face in my memory, but all at once I smelled the musky odor of the sheep shed back in England, when the wool was gathered, and Father was ordering everyone about.

"Well, I think he would be glad we are together now," I said. "And he would not be so concerned about his grand-daughter being attended by one of the good men."

THE MORNING AFTER WE reached the mouth of the Kennebec River, I got up before my children awoke. We had threaded through small islands before anchoring at dusk the night before. I could hear the Kennebec singing as the tide surged into the river. I licked my finger after a wave splashed my hand and the water still tasted salty. John told us that the tide would be carrying us upriver that morning. "We hope to get beyond where the tide carries us before we stop."

Priscilla and I gathered our children at the stern so they would be out of the way, as the captain and all hands kept us moving upriver. We stood with the children, soaking up the changing sights and smells. The Kennebec River was unlike anything at home in Plimoth. Tall trees blotted out sunlight and a ripe, green smell, free of the salt tang that had pervaded earlier, told us we were leaving the sea behind. However, in the marshy eddies that fed the river, familiar red-wing blackbirds clacked and whirred, as they did in the marshes of Cape Cod.

The tallest trees were further from the river now, maple and oaks a buffer between the river and the pines. A shrill cawing announced a flock of crows, careening from the trees to our boat. I laughed at their audacious maneuvering.

"Goody Billington had said there'd be crows in Maine," I smiled.

"Goody Billington?" Priscilla's light blue eyes opened wide. "What on earth would she know about crows in Maine?"

"She knows nothing." I shrugged one shoulder. "I think she was trying to reassure me that moving here would not be so different. And now, here's a flock just like back home."

"Did ye know that a flock of crows is called a 'murder'?" Priscilla was always teaching me. Having been raised in a household with servants who did most of the work, she'd not only had time to learn to read, but also to discuss with her parents topics she shared with me. "Tsk, tsk." she clucked her tongue. "Let's hope some things are different here. Pray that there won't be men like Goody's husband who settled a dispute with murder."

A chill seized my neck. The image of John Billington swinging from the scaffold, head lolling, was complete with the sound of crows. They'd circled the gruesome site even after Billington's body was removed. Obviously, the scent of death was an invitation to feast. Why had I not thought of that when I was with Goody? She must have.

"Elisabeth." Priscilla's hand on my arm brought me back. "Do not dwell on the past. That day is gone. Billington's life was doomed before he was birthed. And, thank God, he did not take our husbands with him." She picked up her youngest, pulling her breast out from her stays to soothe the child.

"We are in a new place now. We'll miss the good and forget the evil until we return home to Plimoth."

The scolding crows circled, then flapped downriver. As we passed a smaller river emptying into the Kennebec, I saw a flash of brilliant blue and white. The big-headed bird, a King-fisher, croaked out a rusty call and then made a buzzing *trrrrr*. She splashed into the water and rose with a small fish in her long bill.

"We have the same birds here," I said with delight. "And, hopefully a lot more beaver."

As the morning passed, our shallop went slower and the riverbanks closed in. We rounded a curve and the sun reflect-ed off something on shore that gleamed like the metal of a gun. Commotion erupted on the shallop as others saw the flash.

Then my young John called out, "Ox!" The dark creature became visible. The man leading it held a gun high with one bare arm, holding onto the ox's rope with the other, his face in the shadow.

I squeezed my eyes shut for a moment to dispel the vision. Did the Abenaki men lead oxen and carry guns? My John had given Black Whale a musket, despite knowing all the colo-nies banned the Indians possessing guns. He and Black Whale agreed it was worth the risk—it was to be kept hidden, but was necessary traveling through dangerous territory. Was this Indian showing his weapon because he feared us, or because the colony of Maine did not enforce the ban?

As we drew closer, the man's face came into view. My John led the cheer when he realized the man was Black Whale! My breath caught as I searched the scene for Attitash. The current carried our shallop forward and finally I could make out the figures behind Black Whale. Attitash and her son ap-peared with her husband. Her brother was behind Attitash and another woman walked beside him. I could not tell who it was and my mind jumped over several unlikely possibilities.

Halloos were called and orders were shouted to trim sail and watch the port side for rocks. At last we were close enough to see the other woman. Her face was familiar but disfigured with scars and an unkempt downcast appearance. I could not affirm it positively, but she appeared to be Attitash's cousin, Seafoam—the one long lost to the Narragansett!

The morning seemed like an entire day as we watched the horizon for a trading post. The river grew more narrow, reeds and trees mingled with rocks on the shore. The path our Indian friends took with their ox often disappeared into the woods and we lost sight as the tide carried us upstream. Gradually, it weakened and the wind coming at us from the west slowed our progress.

Surely, tonight we would be able to sleep on shore. The men were eager to sleep off of the boat, but Priscilla and I required first rights at any bed ashore. No man had to accommodate a growing babe in his belly. It was so crowded sleeping on the shallop that changing positions was nigh impossible.

The sun was high above and hot when a small dot under the trees proved to be the rude cabin that served as the trading post called Koussinoc. I'd been anxious to get off the shallop, but now our new home looked so strange my eagerness dimmed. The two-story fort seemed almost like an imaginary folk-tale, situated as it was in the midst of a wild river and thick forest. John had told me the fort was built the last time he was there, needing space for more men to come. My legs strained as we walked up the rude dock and made our way up the rocky shore. Although I knew it had not been built in a day, John described how his men worked long hours splitting the logs, smoothing them, and mixing the mud and sand to caulk between the clapboards of the first story before they could begin the second.

There were no proper beds, but our husbands made quick work of building the bedsteads, Priscilla and I wound the ropes to support thin pine-needle mattresses. A feather bed or even cornhusk mattress would not be ready until we had the raw materials. Even this rude bed felt like a magnificent mistress's when I could finally lie down. My youngest snuggled with me, so hard against my belly that she and the growing babe must have felt each other kick. The three older children nested in blankets on the floor and John found room to ease his body next to mine. He was sore weary from unloading and hauling in our belongings and supplies and dropped off immediately. At that moment, all I wanted was to be alone with my little family no matter how rough the house. I wrapped myself close to him and joined the rest in sleep.

Attitash:

Seeing Esapett from a distance for such a brief time, after an entire moon apart, made it difficult to watch their small wind canoe disappear up the river. We continued on the path with the ox and reached Koussinoc when Nippa'uus was high.

Their wind canoe was tied up and they had unloaded their belongings. Esapett and I reached our arms out, wanting to embrace each other, but resisted. Too many men I did not know were watching. Taking hands, we quietly touched cheeks. She then stepped back, acknowledging my cousin with a nod of her head. Seafoam stood behind me, one hand clinging to my shoulder for protection and comfort. Esapett's eyes were full of questions, but answers would have to wait until we were alone.

Mosk patted the ox possessively, telling young Jon-owland he could now ride the creature. Mosk did not mention that he'd only been on it with his father, never alone. Young John insisted he could ride also, but before he could try to prove himself, Little Fish intervened. As he rubbed down the ox and turned it over to one of the Strangers, young Jon began describing a sea swimmer they had encountered. It seemed as though he were describing a whale, but if we understood his gestures and the fright in his eyes, it was much larger than any whale I'd seen. Perhaps the boy's wish to impress my son made him grow the whale in his telling.

Esapett took me to see the long-house they called a fort. It was very tall and there were logs that held a floor up in the air above. Steps went from the ground floor room to what they called 'upstairs.'

"We are the first women to live here," Esapett told me. "We each get three rooms and the men who work here sleep altogether in another big room."

Pah-scilla was already there, trying to unpack. She nodded to me, but turned to ask Esapett, "Who is the woman with Attitash?"

Esapett glanced quickly at me, checking to make sure I understood her friend. "Is that Seafoam?"

I nodded and Esapett said something in their words to Pah-scilla. I understood her to say, "That's a relative, who many seasons ago traded herself to the Narragansett for Attitash's sister."

"Do my words tell the truth, Attitash?" Esapett asked me.

"Yea, that is true." I answered in their words so Pah-scilla would understand. To avoid more questions about that terrible time, I said goodbye and went back to my family.

It was a short walk to the Abenaki village, which looked more like our own than I'd expected. The Abenaki women welcomed us and showed us our place in their neesh'wetu— a three-fire longhouse. We had enough room on the sleeping bench for all, but it was crowded. My children would sleep with me, Little Fish and Black Whale in front of us and Seafoam behind. Seafoam and I unpacked, storing our small supplies under the sleeping bench, then joined the Abenaki women. To the Strangers, the Abenaki may have looked like us. The strings wrapped on their legs were similar as was their hair. But their wampum shell ornaments were white, without the beautiful purple cast of our quahog.

They politely greeted us and then continued to chatter with each other. I could understand some words, but one or two words alone carry no meaning.

One of the grandmothers sitting near me leaned over and slowly put her hand towards my belly, her eyes insisting. I allowed this Abenaki grandmother to do what any Wampanoag grandmother would. She closed her eyes, listening, then opened them and spoke slowly so I could understand the words inside her Abenaki accent. "You carry new life."

"Only three moons." I felt a rising of tears within me. My own grandmother would not be with me when I brought my new life to the light. Would this Abenaki grandmother be able to take Grandmother's place? Would the Abenaki grandmother be willing if I wanted her?

Seafoam drew breath quickly and I turned to her. Her own eyes glittered with tears. "Didn't you know?" I asked her quietly. We moved towards the entrance to their longhouse where no one could hear us.

"I have not looked at you," she said, as if looking at me would be an insult. "And you have not looked at me."

The heat of curious eyes warmed my neck. I turned to find the Abenaki grandmother moving slowly toward us. This grandmother saw me not only as someone brought to her home by Strangers. Her look was wise, all-knowing. I'd seen that look when an eagle sat on a branch above me, peering over its golden beak. We had no secrets from this grandmother, only from each other. I put my hands over my belly where my new life's tiny spirit flickered. The grandmother looked away from me and held Seafoam in her gaze.

"Who will bring his hunt for *your* new life?" the grandmother asked Seafoam.

My cousin looked down and her mouth quivered. I put my hand on Seafoam's shoulder and she slumped against me. "Tell me, is this true? Are you carrying new life?" I asked her. Seafoam had said nothing to hint she was breeding, but I did not doubt this grandmother's understanding. My cousin had only been with us one moon, so I had not thought about when her moon flow should come.

"Go, children," the grandmother dismissed us. "You need to talk to each other."

We went back to our place on the sleeping benches and pulled the fur over our heads for privacy. For a long time we just breathed. Finally I asked, "How long since you mated?"

"Mated." Seafoam spat the word. "You mean how long since the pit-faced Stranger took me. No animal mating treats its female like that."

I waited. Our heads were close together; I could hear her heart beating as well as her quick breaths, but our words would not be heard by the Abenaki women.

"I'm not sure," she finally whispered. "I walked so long to escape him. It was already river-ice-gone when I left."

I put my hand gently on her belly. Her bump was no bigger than mine. This new life, evidence of the Stranger's intimate invasion may not be her first. Seafoam had been away a long time. "Seafoam, do you have other children?"

She clutched her breasts with both hands, massaging them. "I had another. He looked like his father—hair like sour red berries. But he did not have the bad-spirit scars on his face that his father carried. I hoped his father would not beat him. I took all the blows for my boy. But it was no use." Seafoam bit her lip. "His father treated him like he treated the dog." She released her breasts and clenched her fists. Her words came out in a low broken voice, "No dog—no woman—no child should be treated like that." My pretty cousin's beauty was long lost. Her eyes were wreathed in dark circles. But she had survived.

"What did he do to you?" I waited. Her eyes flicked to me and then away.

"He ignored us most of the time. He took me without asking when he wanted me, then beat me afterward."

Seafoam's hands trembled. I took them in my own. The scars on her wrists felt wrinkled and dry to me.

"Are these burns?"

She nodded, sobbing softly and I drew her head to mine. "He took a stick to my son's back when the boy bothered him. I knew my son could endure that. But when the Stranger took a burning stick to him…." Her voice trailed off. I did not need to ask if the boy survived. I could only hope he died quickly. Bad spirits bring a fire that burns up a little child as if he were kindling.

Seafoam knew she need not explain. She clutched herself and rocked back and forth. "I ran away to save my new child."

I held her until the sobs finally lost their strength and we sat together quietly. My mind saw only my cousin when she was young and pretty—when she believed her life would continue to be filled with people who loved her.

"Seafoam, we will give your new life a chance."

WHEN BLACK WHALE AND I WERE AT LAST ABLE to find a place under a tree near the river, he put his arm around me, but did not urge me further. Our children played on the bank and we both kept watch. Our hearts beat the same beat. I told him that Seafoam carried new life, sprung from the seed of a cruel Stranger. That was enough for now. My husband would listen when I was ready to unburden later.

We sat watching the river flow to the sea, the tide no longer reaching its long tongue upriver. I leaned against my husband and put my hand on his, which held me against him. He squeezed back and his strength comforted me. As Nippa'uus slowly settled into the west, our children sat nearer to us, their chatter a familiar sound—like birds chirping at dusk. Black Whale released my fingers and moved his fingers up to trace my cheek. I kissed his fingers, grateful for the small intimacy.

5

August 1632
Koussinoc
Kennebec, Maine

Elisabeth:

When I got up to use the piss pot in the middle of the night, John sat up.

"Do ye still have trouble sleeping, Love?"

"It's much better, but there's only so much room in my body." Truth be told, I had lost weight on the voyage and my hip bones were poking out, surrounding the swell of my womb.

My husband went back to sleep, but I lay awake wondering about Attitash's new household. Her cousin, Seafoam, had been with the Narragansett for ten years, I thought. That was about the time I was truly wed to John. Would Attitash now have to share her husband with her cousin? I knew Hopamoch had two wives. I traced John's neck where it nested in his powerful shoulders. Could Attitash ever take a sister-wife? Would Black Whale want one? Would my John wish he could have two wives? When we met, I was thirteen and

John twenty-eight. I knew he'd at least kissed a maid or two. The thought made me ill then. Now I wondered if he ever yearned for some woman he'd known back in England. I tried to suppress evil thoughts about my husband—wondering if he would want me to share him with another. John shifted and pulled me close to him. His breathing went back to its slow sleepy rhythm. I drew my own breaths with his and banished the evil imaginations. It could curdle my blood to even think such sin. I carried a babe and only God would know what that would do to my babe.

I buried my head in the curve of my husband's shoulder and prayed fiercely to God to take away these hideous thoughts. Let me be Attitash's friend and John's wife without the pollution of such ideas.

PEPE-WARR, WHITE FROST MOON

Attitash:

Seafoam and I were drying squash at a fire near the field when Black Whale came running back from a hunt. "Trouble! I am going with Jon-owland to the river," he said between deep breaths. Without waiting for our questions, he stuck a club in his sash, arrows in his quiver, and slinging his bow, ran off. My cousin made an obvious effort to remain calm, breathing deeply and blowing out her breath. But her shoulders were hunched and her lips were tight. She was as fragile as the new fern after being stepped on. Every little incident disturbed her.

"It's probably a moose or a bear," I assured her. The Abenaki would be there to help should an angry bear threaten, but we knew Black Whale could probably handle that by himself. Only a snarler, which the Strangers called "mountain lion," would be difficult for one man to handle. The snarlers could run fast and jump.

I looked to where Mosk had been playing with sticks near the fire, but no one was there. He must have followed the Abenaki children somewhere. I called out, but no answer.

"You go towards the river to look for him," Seafoam said. "I'll stay here to watch the fire."

I could hear the river tumbling behind the trees when I finally found the children. He was at the fenced meadow with the Strangers' ox, feeding bits of squash to it—showing off to a group of Abenaki children. I sent them all to the longhouse with strict instructions to stay with the grandmothers until we knew what the trouble was. It didn't take me long to return to the fire. Seafoam was gone. She would never leave a burning fire! Between our men at the river, the children, and now my cousin, my heart was lurching in all directions. I started back to the longhouse when I heard crashing in the bushes. Was it a wolf? A bear? A stranger? I drew my knife and crouched, trying to understand the sound. A cry told me it was not an animal.

"Seafoam?" I shrieked. Another crashing—this one behind me. It was a Stranger, the one with hair so yellow it resembled the man who's grave the first Strangers desecrated. This Yellow Hair was very much alive, the one Jon-owland called "Moses-Ta-bot." He pushed in front of me, calling out "Halt!"

The long glinting nose of a firestick parted the bushes. Then a flame burst as a fireball whizzed over my head.

"Cease and desist!" Moses-Ta-bot called out. "Let go of that maid." He motioned to me and I jumped into the bushes, squatting down where I could still see him as he fumbled with his bandoliers, loading his musket while keeping an eye on the bushes. "There are reinforcements behind me, Hocking."

I was not sure what he meant, but another fireball flew by us. The ugly face of a Stranger appeared above the firestick. Hair the color of sour berries covered his mouth as well as his head. His face was marked by pits, the kind left by the bad spirits which killed so many of my people. Pit-Face held the firestick with one hand, his other was clenched around Seafoam's neck, bowing her head down so she could not see me. Moses-Ta-bot shot above their heads, as Seafoam's captor ducked, shoving her down. I rushed forward, knife in hand, and stabbed Hocking's shoulder, causing him to let go of Seafoam and his firestick. Blood oozed out. Moses-Ta-bot grabbed the Stranger's weapon and I grabbed Seafoam.

"Run," Moses-Talbot said. We did not look back, but ran to the river to find Black Whale and Jon-owland. We were still trying to explain to Jon-owland what happened when Moses arrived dragging Pit-Face with a rope around his torso. Blood soaked his shirt.

Jon-owland spat on the ground when he saw the captive. "I should have known it was you, Hocking."

I could not understand everything said, but enough to realize that Pit-Face was a man called Hocking and was from an enemy tribe. Black Whale watched with us, all our weapons at the ready, as Moses-Talbot and Jon-owland put Pit-Face in a dugout canoe and took him out to a small wind canoe anchored on the river. A few men sat there, firesticks pointing down. From their gestures toward Seafoam and me, I realized with a jolt to my gut that Pit-Face's men must know Seafoam.

I led my cousin away. She was shaking like the white-bark leaf. "Is that him?" I asked Seafoam.

She trembled so that her teeth clattered. "Ahhe," She put her hands on her belly.

Elisabeth:

When I heard the 'halloo' that told me it was safe to go to the river, I ran to find out what happened.

"Robert Hocking is a poacher," John told me after Hocking's boat with his men pointing their muskets at us, had finally gone downriver. I knew that rich men in England were behind the attempt to take the timber and beaver trade from us, so I was not surprised. Now, with the poachers' shallop gone, John stopped to feed and groom our ox. It was agitated from the musket firings and tossed his head when John tried to use the curry comb on its neck.

As I waited for the ox to settle down, I had to ask, "Why did ye let the poacher go? Surely he'll return. Could he not be held in our stocks?"

John kept working the comb and did not look up. "We don't have many reserves here. The men in Plimoth are two weeks sailing away. And we don't know who Hocking brought with him, hidden out of sight. It could be a trap. If we put Hocking in our little stockade, then two boatloads of his men could show up and raid us."

I knew we were far from home but had not realized how precarious our position was. Using the other brush on the beast's withers, I talked in the sing-song way my husband had taught me. Calming the ox calmed me, but I still had a lot of questions. "Is this Hocking the same poacher ye were sent to deal with or is he from another financier in England?"

"I believe it's all the same greedy lot back home." John put his hand on the back of its leg, touching a muscle that made the ox lift his hoof. John steadied the hoof on his leg as he concentrated on picking out small stones. I held my questions. When he finished with the hoof, John put his hand on its neck, soothing the beast. Still without looking at me, he asked, "Is Attitash's cousin breeding? She looks swollen in the belly despite being very thin in her limbs and face."

I was surprised he'd looked closely at the Indian maid. "Yea, Seafoam is a few months gone, according to Attitash." I held my own swollen belly—seven months of babe growing. "She seems to be as far gone as Attitash."

"If she is, Hocking could be coming to claim his child. Is she too far gone to be Black Whale's?"

I swallowed the bile that rose at such a suggestion. "Mayhap, I'm not sure. Must you count months?"

"If not Hocking's, whose is it?" He gave the ox a final pat and looked at me. "Ye know her father has two wives—as does Massasowet. Black Whale and Attitash are heathen, too."

How did my husband know what I was thinking? Could he read my mind like the papers he wrote?

"You two have been friends for many years and I know how much she means to thee," he continued. "But ye must not hope that the heathen will follow God's commandment not to commit adultery, Dear Heart."

Long after our children slept, I lay spooned with my belly pushing into John's strong back. He breathed the slow breaths of the sound sleeper. I traced the muscles of his arms, feeling them tense as I touched them. Moving to his shoulders, I used the heel of my hand to push the tight muscles holding his neck. John moaned softly in pleasure and seemed to rouse. But weariness overtook him and he slumped again in deep sleep. I turned onto my back, but that position was impossible with my growing babe pressing on my innards. Shifting again, I settled my back against John's. My fingers tingled with a memory, but it was not the memory of touching my husband. It was of wanting to touch another man. When Moses Talbot was showing my son how to use the sail ropes, I'd had to suppress the urge to touch Talbot's arms. Mayhap my prayers should be for my own soul. Surely lust for someone else can creep into the most loving marriage and threaten it.

Attitash:

That night I moved from my place by Black Whale and slept by Seafoam. When Seafoam woke in the middle of the night, I held her.

"Feel my baby," Seafoam whispered. "She wants to live."
Putting my hand on her belly, I felt the hard bulge. "She will."

A few days later, we were both mashing the sour berries

when Moses-Ta-bot came to our fire. He greeted me politely, with down-cast eyes. "I hope she is better, I have not seen her since—the attempt," he said in their words, then glanced quickly at Seafoam. "Kwe."

Having used all his Wampanoag words by saying 'hello,' he went back to his own words. "Feeling better, Mistress?"

Seafoam smiled. She knew some of the Strangers' words from being with Hocking, but she turned to me. "What is 'bet-ta?"

"Healing," I told her in our words.

I stayed by Seafoam as Moses asked how she felt, patting his own belly.

She giggled and responded, "I fine, catabatash."

Moses looked at me and I told him, "Catabatash is, 'Thank you'."

Moses-Ta-bot tried saying it, which prompted more giggles. He offered a small beaker to Seafoam. "I saved a little ale from my ration, mistress," he said. "I know you don't usually drink it, but it will soothe your nerves."

"Don't give that to her!" I commanded. From the corner of my eye, I saw an Abenaki woman approaching. "Go!" I told Moses-Ta-bot. "Don't ask why. Just go." He hesitated, so I waved my hands, shooing him like I would a turkey in my path. I did not have words or time to explain to Moses-Ta-bot why it was forbidden for a Stranger-man to come visit Seafoam. But Ta-bot should have known already that their strong drink brings very bad spirits to us.

The Abenaki woman said nothing, but her eyes followed Moses-Ta-bot as he put the beaker in his bag and left. After supper that night, the grandmother who headed their council found me as I was scraping out pots with sand.

"Your sister must get a husband."

I paused, waiting to see if she was offering an Abenaki man. "She is not my sister, we are different clans. Her father is my Otter clan. She is her mother's Beaver Clan."

The grandmother let my words land on her ears but did not seem to allow them into her mind. "She will be your sister-wife. Your husband must take her. She needs a husband now, to heal and to keep the Cloth-man from taking her child if it lives to see the light."

I kept my face still, not allowing the Abenaki grandmother to see the shudder that rippled through my body at the thought of sharing Black Whale with my cousin.

Elisabeth:

Priscilla and her John were sitting with us after supper. The fire burned low but was needed now that the sun set early and a chill was in the air. The men had been at work fixing up the rooms in the fort for more than a month. It was a grand building—two stories with common kitchen and sitting on the ground floor and a stable with its outside door on one end.

Priscilla and I were chatting when I heard John Alden say to my John, "It seems Talbot is sniffing up the other Indian maid."

Priscilla glanced at me, her blue eyes sparking. "Do forgive my husband's crude description of Attitash's sister."

"Her cousin," I replied, as if the kinship were more significant than John Alden's description. Attitash had explained their clans were different, but I also understood Seafoam's father was brother to Attitash's mother. I realized I only pointed out cousin instead of sister because my John had raised the bigamy issue. I leaned toward Priscilla so our children would not hear my query. "Has your John seen Moses with Seafoam?'

Priscilla shrugged. "My John is like the old wives. He loves to gossip." She chuckled. "He did mention that one of the other lads said Talbot was taking a healing gift to the Indian he rescued from Hocking."

"Do ye know what he took? I didn't give him any remedies."

"Evidently, Talbot took ale to the maid."

Since Priscilla had no knowledge, I asked my husband. Needless to say neither of us were happy with the answer. My John tried to explain that Moses Talbot was young and simply uninformed. "Bradford gave their King Massasowet strong drink—aquavit. So what's the harm in a little ale?"

"Don't ye remember how their King broke out in a sweat from just one quaff? God didn't make them able to hold strong drink."

John raised an eyebrow. "A little ale? Ye do protest too much."

"Mayhap, but Talbot sets a bad example," I answered. "Most of the other men would not be as considerate with a maid they believe to be Satan's consort. They would see Talbot befriending her and think she was their prey, too."

"My men will be hard to control regardless. There are few enough of thy sex for my men to chase after. Ye might have noticed that Alden's young daughters and ours are the only single Christian women here." John left care of our daughters to me, but his protection was fierce. Especially for our Desire, since her budding nipples showed impending womanhood.

"Talbot's attention to Seafoam might prevent him from setting a bad example with our young maids," he continued. "Ye have no doubt observed that Talbot is a lusty young man."

My cheeks flamed with the accuracy of his words. 'Twas true that Moses Talbot was pleasant to look at and to be with. He had the firm body of a man well under forty. He reminded me of my John ten years ago when we first met. And he was kind to all us women and children. With a little seasoning, he would be capable of becoming a leader, too—and lose the eager assumption that he could solve every problem. I threw another log on the fire and blew on the embers. It shamed me to realize that a man I'd noticed might someday want my daughter. The fire flared up and I wiped the drops of sweat from my brow. "Can we just talk about how to soothe this situation with Talbot and Seafoam?"

October/Pepe'warr, white frost moon

Attitash:

Seafoam had set her eyes on Black Whale when she and I were young, before I was sure of his desire for me. That old memory came roaring back as I sat at the fire listening to the grandmother explain the plan that Black Whale should take Seafoam as a sister-wife. I tried to keep my eyes down, but when I heard no objection, I glanced at my husband's face. Not only was there no refusal, but some acceptance on his features.

He joined me at the fire later and I waited for him to speak. He only took my hand. I almost pulled away but let him hold on gently. I did not want his hands touching Seafoam, but the grandmothers had spoken. Black Whale knew it was not his place to object to the Grandmothers. He was the only choice for Seafoam. My reluctance to accept this had made me wonder if Little Fish could become her husband instead, but he was so much younger, and had not yet gone through his vision quest.

I wanted to ask if Black Whale found the prospect agreeable, but I was not sure what his answer would be. Better to wonder than to be forced to hear the truth.

Seafoam was the one who objected, not to the grandmother, but later to me. We were on our way to carry water from the river when she voiced her refusal.

"I do not need a man. I could not lie with a man now. My child could be harmed," she said with fervor.

I put my birch-bucket down and took her arm. I knew the Grandmothers—and perhaps Black Whale—would insist that Seafoam did need him.

"Ye only need him to protect thee, not share thy body," I

told Seafoam. "Ye must have a man to keep away the rutting Strangers." She still did not look at me, so I continued. "Do not say this to spare my feelings, Seafoam. Black Whale can protect thee and thy child."

She did not resist my hand on her arm. "I do not want thy husband. Why should I take a man I do not want?"

Seafoam raised her eyes to meet mine briefly. I could not read her thoughts, but she looked wary. "When we are back home, my brother, thy child's Clan Uncle, can take care of us both," she said.

"But who knows when we'll be back home again. Ye and thy child must be safe now." Was she rejecting my husband because he had not been kind to her? Or had he made advances? I could not raise my fears to her now. If either one were true, Seafoam would deny any such thing to protect my knowing. If she refused Black Whale, I would not have to share him. But that left her with no protection. We continued walking back to the Abenaki longhouse.

During the day, I watched Seafoam and Black Whale. There was little to see. They rarely spoke to each other, and then only brief conversations. No hint of hostility or interest either way. I spent a restless night sleeping by my husband. My growing child was a moving bundle against my inner body as well as a barrier between us. Seafoam was nearly as big as I, so I knew she tossed and turned herself.

Next morning, Seafoam came with me to relieve ourselves in the women's pit. I decided to ask her directly why she did not want Black Whale. The blank look on her face revealed my question was not one she'd considered.

"It has nothing to do with Black Whale—ye know I have always thought ye got the good husband. I do not want him now because he could not protect me."

"Why? He's strong and can use his club better than any man."

"Attitash, listen." Seafoam folded her arms, looking like a

grandmother herself in her bearing, despite her youth. "That Stranger who rescued me—Ta-bot. He would be a better shield."

"Ye would take a stranger to shield against your husband?" I could hardly swallow, her suggestion was so unexpected. Surely after Pit-Face Hocking, Seafoam had had enough of the Strangers.

"Mata, Pit-Face is the father, but he is not my *husband*." Seafoam spat out our word for a man who would live at our fire, take care of us and give us children. Seafoam put her hand on her swollen belly and caught the sob that escaped her throat. "I carry a child seeded by a Stranger, that is true, but only another Stranger could keep that scum Pit-Face from taking my baby away. If I have a Stranger protecting me, then Pit-Face Hocking might not lay hands on me." Seafoam rose from the women's pit. "He has helped me with carrying water and chopping wood and never once laid a hand on me," Seafoam said. My cousin looked away from my questioning stare, then smiled. "I don't tell you everything I do, Attitash. Even though you think you must look after me like one of thy children."

Seafoam might be right about Ta-bot, but she was wrong that I treated her like a child. "I will talk to Esapett," I told her. "Esapett and her husband would know whether we could trust this Ta-bot." We walked back without more words between us.

SEAFOAM'S PLAN SAT IN MY MIND like a night-terrors dream. Would anything keep Pit-Face away? It seemed impossible to me that she could keep this Ta-bot close enough to be protection without having to succumb to being taken to his bed. Maybe Seafoam was too swollen with new life now for Ta-bot, but there were no women here except Esapett and Pahscilla—both with husbands. Stranger-men were known to take whatever they could find. We could not dismiss Ta-bot being tempted to take Seafoam. But setting Ta-bot up as her pretend husband would not be an easy act. The grandmothers would have to be persuaded that it was necessary to have this Stranger close to us. I did not know if there had been other Strangers mating with Abenaki, like the yellow hair I'd met so long ago who seemed to be father of the little Wampanoag boy. That tragedy lay forever in my heart. If Ta-bot could be trusted, he might be able to protect Seafoam and her infant.

As I tried putting words in my mouth to explain to the grandmothers, I realized I also needed to talk with Black Whale. He would have many objections to a Stranger being Seafoam's mate. But he might also be disappointed that Seafoam did not want him.

I found him at his weir, pulling in the net that held a few fish. I used as few words as possible. "Seafoam wants a Stranger to protect her baby. Ta-bot seems least likely to misuse her. I will ask the Abenaki Grandmothers Council."

Waiting for my husband to express his opinion, I observed his habit of crossing his arms, the glint in his eyes dimmer as he thought. The fish thrashed about in the weir, but he ignored them.

"Are you disappointed?" I asked hesitantly.

"Disappointed? Why would I be disappointed?"

I knew better than to answer his question honestly. It would show my girlish possessiveness of my husband.

Black Whale almost smiled. "You're enough woman for me to handle now." His hands were wet, but he patted my bottom anyway. And I was glad. A little lump in my throat slid away and I took his hand and pulled it to my waist.

Black Whale sighed, "It would be a relief not to be responsible for all Seafoam's needs, but it's an abominable choice for her. Are you sure she must have another stranger, after all she's been through?"

"Seafoam says it takes a Stranger to keep Pit-Face away."

Black Whale pursed his lips. I could see the struggle

between his pride in his ability to fight and his understanding that Seafoam's predicament was not easily solved by two men fighting. "She may be right, but Seafoam knows she could be harmed no matter who tries to protect her." He picked up the weir and slid the mess of fish into his woven bag, then pulled it closed. The fish desperately continued their futile thrashing.

Elisabeth:

It did not take long to persuade John of the need to have one of his men safeguard Seafoam. At first, I could not believe Attitash was serious about deliberately throwing Talbot and Seafoam together when he had shown his lack of judgement by giving her ale. And I had no answer to her question regarding whether Talbot could be trusted not to bed Seafoam. I did understand the urgency of Seafoam's situation, however, with her babe due soon and Hocking threatening her. When I put the question to my husband, I suggested one of his other men become her escort. "Attitash told me that the Grandmothers' Council does not want her to live with Talbot."

"Do ye really place credence in the old women?" John's dismissive vehemence did not surprise me, but it did make me feel like my sex deserved more credence than even my beloved husband gave us. I turned my face to the handiwork in my lap and listened to his continued discourse.

"But Talbot likes the maid, and he would not harm her. My other men would not treat her with mercy." John tended to form his opinions without mulling. And, truth be told, I often found he was right. This time, however, it did not seem certain to me.

So it was that both of us took Moses Talbot aside and put the difficult task to him. He must protect Seafoam, accompany her when she leaves their longhouse, give her no ale, and no bedding.

"Ye must not allow thy lust to be unleashed, Moses." My

John's eyes glinted bright green, revealing his anger at the position he was put in because of Hocking.

"Are you saying not ever? Even after she delivers the babe?" Talbot's question did not reassure me.

"Let's get through the next few months," John replied. "Can ye promise me that? Look into thy heart, Lad. If ye can't promise, Black Whale might take her as second wife, but when her babe is born...."

John did not finish the thought. Attitash had told me Hocking kept Seafoam as a wife before she escaped. Moses Talbot had kept Hocking from stealing Seafoam back and must have suspected that the child she carried was Hocking's.

Moses drew a deep breath. "I will not touch her or give her ale."

He and John shook hands, then John added, "After she's suckled her child, if ye still want her and think she wants thee, we'll check the lay of the land—her land and ours—before ye consider whom ye lie with."

Now Moses smiled. A small, shy smile. It would be months or more, but he seemed to think his passion would continue.

It was evident that Talbot had little realization of Seafoam's damaged body and damaged heart. And little understanding of the chasm between her ways and ours. I started to voice caution, but the look on John's face silenced me. I realized, as so often in this new world, we needed an immediate answer to a dangerous situation. Having no answer, we must place our trust in the Lord. Only He could see the future for a heathen woman and Christian man.

Attitash:

It was agreed by all that Seafoam would remain in the Longhouse until her child was brought to light. The Strangers' big fort, Koussinoc, had room for everyone.

Esapett brought her fifth child to the light in their room.

Pah-scilla was with her when she delivered. Jon-owland gave the good news to Black Whale and we all rejoiced.

"They will soon rejoice for us," I told Seafoam.

BOTH OF US WERE SWOLLEN UP like pumpkins when Seafoam's belly began to squeeze her baby out. The grandmothers prepared a healing ceremony in their moon lodge. Seafoam accepted the herb teas, the soothing breaths of sweet grass and sage. She seemed to be sleeping when her face suddenly contorted with pain. She clutched her belly and groaned as blood oozed out between her legs. I looked to the grandmothers, they did nothing.

"She's losing her baby!" I cried out.

The grandmothers did not speak. One of them bathed Seafoam's face, telling her, "This baby is not one of us. Not one of you. It is a Stranger's," a Grandmother said. "It is best for the bad spirits to take it."

I dared not look the Abenaki grandmother in the face. If only we were home with our own grandmothers. My grandmother's scent came to me, her own peculiar combination of sweet grass, sage and the teas she loved. Her voice was in my ear, reminding me vividly of the sick little boy I found with the Yellow Hair father. This boy had loved his father and when they both died we buried them with full Wampanoag ceremony. The violation of their grave by our Strangers still hung in my heart. Reaching into the basket kept in the moon lodge, I took out a large moss poultice and stuffed it against her woman-place. Putting my hands gently on Seafoam's belly, I told her, "Your baby is still moving."

Seafoam bit her lips as another pain wracked her. I held the jar so she could drink water. Slowly the pain left her face.

"Why do you want this baby to live?" The grandmother asked me.

I stroked Seafoam's face. "This baby is her clan, not the man's who stuck his seed in her."

"You Wampanoag have the Strangers' ways now," the grandmother said and blew her breath out harshly. "She is yours to deliver."

If I had not gone through my own delivery of my lost new life and then my son Mosk, I could not have done it. By chanting prayers and providing strength in my hands for her legs to push against, Seafoam brought her little girl to the light. The baby was tiny. I put her to Seafoam's breast. It seemed she did not have the strength to suckle. I tweaked Seafoam's nipple till it stood up stiff and was easy to insert in the tiny mouth, then I massaged the little cheeks until the infant managed a few sucks. Seafoam kept the little girl against her own body, every few minutes she gave the child another few sucks.

In a short while, Seafoam closed her eyes. Telling her to sleep, I took the baby. She was smaller than my Mosk, bigger than my lost one. This baby did not look like one of ours but more like Esapett's babies when they were born. Instead of a thatch of thick dark hair, Seafoam's baby had hardly any. Her skin was faded light brown, not quite the sick no-color of Strangers. Seafoam opened her eyes as I tucked her daughter in next to her.

"She's mine, no matter what she looks like," Seafoam murmured.

"Ahhe, she's yours," I answered.

"Don't let anyone else near her." Seafoam closed her eyes again and spoke in a whisper. "We must get her away from eyes that see a bad-spirit baby."

"As soon as we have a new place to live," I promised.

After two Nippa'uus rising and setting, the baby's cheeks were no longer shrunken. Seafoam was back on her feet, now trusting that her child might survive. I thanked all the Spirits that Seafoam's encounter with Pit-Face Hocking did not end with a fireball killing the child.

Seafoam was allowed to stay with her baby in the moon lodge for a few days. She and the baby, which she named Red Berry, moved into the Neesh'-wetu without a plan for where they would move to later. It was too complicated since it involved living with Moses—a Stranger. Esapett told me that Jon-owland and Moses were trying to decide where he and Seafoam could live. I'd learned that the Strangers' decisions were made by men even when the decision was about women. I still puzzled over this practice in the Strangers' life. Esapett seemed strong, but she and the other women either did not want to make decisions or were forced to sit back and wait.

Moses wanted to build a small wetu like ours next to Koussinoc. However, Seafoam could not live there alone with him. She would be subject to harsh criticism from the Abenaki women as well as from our people.

"I have to live with you and Black Whale," Seafoam insisted. "Just for a few moons. It's the only way."

Elisabeth:

Praise God all our new babes were delivered safely. My delivery went even more easily than my first four. Our new daughter, Lydia, was small and slipped out quickly. A week after Lydia was born, and days after Seafoam delivered, Black Whale stopped at our house to tell us that Attitash also delivered a healthy daughter, she named Nipi—Water.

"She will leave the moon lodge tomorrow," he told us. The next morning, I pulled on my cloak to walk through the cool frost of early autumn to their village. I found Attitash and Seafoam sitting outside the longhouse, both their babes sucking happily. It made my belly flutter uncomfortably to see that Seafoam's babe looked more like my own.

"Has Moses Talbot seen the babe yet?" I asked.

Seafoam and Attitash exchanged glances. "The grandmothers

won't let him come to their longhouse," Attitash told me. "Sea-foam met him by the river a few days ago to show him the child."

I looked at Seafoam for a clue of whether or not it went well, but she kept her head bent down. If there had been any doubt that Moses understood Hocking had spawned the babe, he would know for certain after seeing the child, that he was part Christian.

"Tell your man that Moses and I want a wetu near your big-house," Seafoam murmured.

Trying not to show my surprise, I agreed. In fact, when I returned home and asked my John, he nodded quietly. "I was going to tell you—they want to build an Indian house near Koussinoc."

"When were ye going to tell me?' I demanded.

John paused, then said, "It will provoke gossip."

I gave him my darkest look. "Do ye really think I am a gossip?"

"Nay! But I didn't want to burden thee with keeping a secret."

"So, I learned it from Seafoam."

John took my hand. "I was going to tell thee after I talked to Black Whale and Little Fish to make sure they approved of this arrangement."

This confused me, as it seemed Seafoam and Attitash would be making this plan, but I knew John expected the men to make the decision. "And did ye ever have this discussion?"

"Yea, but only this morning."

"Who will live in it? When will they start building?"

"They told me all of them—Seafoam, Talbot, Black Whale, Attitash, Little Fish, and the three children will live there." He said. "And they will begin building their wetu—as they call it—as soon as possible, before the snow gets any deeper."

But how could Moses Talbot actually live with them? Even though Attitash and Black Whale were dear friends, I could not manage to sleep in the same house with the entire household. Moses would be the only Christian in the house.

ATTITASH AND SEAFOAM and their little daughters were busy in their new home. I did not see them for two weeks as they stayed in the Abenaki village while the poles were cut and bent to form the arch to support their house near our fort. When I finally visited them, the women were making mats for the inside of the house. Black Whale and Little Fish were adding bark to the outside, the fierce winds already brought more cold and snow. Meanwhile, the family would have to remain in the Abenaki longhouse, and Moses with the other men in our fort.

During that time, Moses was restless, coming to our room to ask if I had seen Seafoam. John reassured him that no evil men would venture through this deep snow. The snow blew so hard that even John stayed in the house most of the time.

6

1633

Attitash:

Moon faded from full to a slim hook, but the cold-sky spirits kept us from finishing our new wetu. At last, the snow ended and Nippa'uus shone brightly. The Abenaki grandmothers were uncertain whether we should all move into a wetu near Koussinoc. They looked a little more kindly on Red Berry, Seafoam's baby, once she started to smile, but still insisted that she live elsewhere.

"Do you have to live with her there, too?" a grandmother asked me. "Whoever planted his seed in Seafoam will come to get her, so I understand why she needs be safer living by the Strangers. But you don't need to stay there."

"We can't leave her with the Ta-bot man alone," I replied.

The grandmother nodded. She took my hand and stroked all the rough spots that marked the hand of a full-grown woman.

"Come to our Neesh'wetu if you need to," she said.

"I won't leave her alone."

"No, but if a Stranger takes her away, you should come back to us."

Ta-bot brought a pallet made of corn shucks and laid it out on the sleeping bench at the back of our round wetu. The shucks rustled every time he turned over, so none of us slept. We might not have anyway. I was used to the Strangers' smell after all these circles of the seasons, but to wake up in the dark of night and still smell their sour smell was not something I could ever get used to. Little Fish, Black Whale, Mosk, my baby Nipi, and I were on one side—close enough to hear Ta-bot's breathing. We would hear him if he ever got up and moved to where Seafoam and Red Berry slept on the other side.

Ta-bot spent all day working with Jon-owland. Little Fish and Black Whale showed our friends how to mend the weir by the spring when the fish got tangled in the nets and tore them.

When the men came home that night, Ta-bot's presence disturbed our dogs. Mowi and Suki—both descended from our original dogs—had not objected to Ta-bot outside, but growled when he came in. The dogs expressed what I felt.

Ta-bot was quiet, sitting at his place on the bench honing his knife. When the dogs settled down, he took a bit of meat from his bowl and placed it on his knee, then looked away. Suki approached cautiously. Mowi, the bigger dog, hung back next to Black Whale. Ta-bot kept his eyes averted. Suki crept forward slowly, snagged the meat, then retreated.

Our son Mosk, laughed, then called Suki and petted her, a proud grin on his face. "She's my family's, not yours."

Ta-bot smiled at Mosk, then put another piece of meat on his knee.

"Don't give the dog all your stew," Seafoam told Ta-bot. "You'll have to bring us more turkey." She brought a ladle of stew and poured it in Ta-bot's bowl. I noticed Seafoam was not careful to keep her hand from touching his as she lifted the ladle. Nor did Ta-bot avert his eyes from her face. He ate all the stew without giving Suki more.

After a few morsels at meals, Suki approached Ta-bot as soon as he came in, even when he did not take from his bowl to tempt her. I no longer felt my belly flip when Ta-bot entered in our wetu. But I still watched him and Seafoam carefully for signs that he might force himself upon her. Had my own feelings allowed me to put her in danger? I was grateful that Ta-bot, not my husband, was her protector, but I worried that she might need protection from Ta-bot himself.

When I asked Seafoam, she insisted Ta-bot did not approach her any closer when I was not there. "It's like there's a cocoon around me, like I'm a caterpillar. Maybe he's waiting for me to turn into a butterfly." A small smile warmed her face. "Meanwhile, he won't try to intrude."

"Do you want him to?"

She did not answer, which I understood was an answer, but not one she wanted to tell me.

Black Whale and Little Fish were preparing for Little Fish's vision quest, practicing survival skills and praying for courage. My little brother had now lived for three-hands of the circle of seasons. I tried to believe that Little Fish was truly a man, ready to take the name our Otter Clan uncle gave him. If so, he would return from his vision quest as Fish Hawk. If not, the storm spirits would claim him. It was the same for every young man, but the chance this could happen to my brother, felt like a sharp icicle hanging above our heads.

"Ta-bot will be the only man left in the wetu when I take your brother to the place where he will meet the Spirits," Black Whale told me. "Will you and Seafoam be safe, or should you go back to the Abenaki home?"

"Seafoam wants him here to guard her against Pit-face. Even in the winter."

Black Whale took my hands. "You must watch. Your cousin's heart is too slippery. She looks at Ta-bot with mating eyes."

"How can you tell? Are you now an expert on Seafoam? Or on mating eyes?"

Black Whale laughed as though I were merely joking. "You know more about that than I do, so I trust you to watch her and Ta-bot."

MANY TIMES WE'D STAYED in our home village waiting when young men went on their vision quest. But this time it was my brother. This time we were not back at our home. Now we were with Abenaki. And this time the white storm spirits filled the whole sky with whirling clouds—beautiful in a single snowflake, but fierce when joined.

Once I'd feared that my brother would not survive, or not grow strong enough for a Vision Quest. Had Esapett not rescued him from the river, he would have drowned when he was a small boy. Now Little Fish was tall and strong. Since we came to the Abenaki, he'd taken his share of the responsibilities. I believed he was now prepared to gain full manhood. Black Whale praised my brother, almost becoming like a clan uncle to him since Uncle Red Hawk was so far away. Little Fish and Black Whale provided meat for us and enough beaver and other furs to keep us clothed and sheltered and enough to give to Jon-owland.

The morning my brother left on his quest, the Abenaki sachem and Black Whale chanted their prayers, letting him breathe the sweet grass and sage smoke. They reminded my brother of the sacred light inside him. We all sang too, giving him the courage of our People.

Nippa'uus gave the snow such glaring light that once Black Whale left him at the meeting place, my brother would have no trouble seeing. He would check the rocks, trees and streams to follow the Abenaki Sachem's directions to the place where the spirits would test him.

The wind began to howl in the middle of the night. By next morning the snow spirits blocked out Nippa'uus.

Mid-morning, Black Whale's whistle carried through the wind and alerted me that he was back. Though I crawled to the opening flap and looked out, I could not see him through the blankets of white until he was close enough to touch.

"Oh," I cried out, laughing from the shock and delight. Before he came inside, Black Whale shook his furs. "You are home," I murmured.

Black Whale laughed. "Glad you recognized me, Wife." He came in and found a place by the fire. "I left Little Fish at the meeting place for his quest and then checked my traps," Black Whale pulled off his furs. "But the storm spirits kept me from checking all them."

My face felt stiff, trying not to show my concern. If Little Fish could not fight the storm spirits, we would find my brother's remains when the snow melted. My heart felt like each beat was a cold slow drip of a frozen stream as it oozed over the rocks.

Black Whale pulled me against him. "He knows what to do." Wrapped in my husband's arms, I breathed in his hope for Little Fish.

The fourth day of the vision quest, the storm spirits added deep cold to the wind and snow. I knew Little Fish would break the hard water and fill his birch-bark kettle to heat over the fire he made. He had plenty of sharp rocks to scrape together, making a spark for a fire. He would build a shelter from supplies he carried on his sled as he snow-shoed to where he would meet with the spirits. Morning was almost like evening. Dark except for the white whirling against our faces when we ventured out. I tried to picture Little Fish safe inside a cave or in a shelter beside a rock.

That night, my dreams brought me Little Fish. My brother was sleeping in his shelter. I could see him and could hear what he heard—the slow heavy breathing of a cougar, interrupted by an occasional low snarl. It was as though I were in the shelter with Little Fish. Then I was outside, looking at the beautiful qumuno, as we call cougars, lying on a rock a few paces from the shelter. I did not feel afraid because I knew Little Fish was not afraid. But when I woke from my dream, fear gripped me like the harsh cold outside. I listened to everyone breathing. My husband, my baby, my son, Seafoam, her baby, and Moses Ta-bot breathing. But all this breathing was not as loud as was the qumuno's.

Elisabeth:

A banging on the door startled us as we sat by the big fire in the common room. John opened it to find Black Whale. Brushing snow from his furs and stomping, Black Whale came inside and sat by the fire. The men gathered near backed away to make room for him. "You know Little Fish is on a vision quest."

We both nodded.

"I go to meeting place. See if Little Fish there." Black Whale said. I knew it was rude to look into his eyes, but I caught a glimpse of fear in the clench of his jaw.

"Attitash dream her brother with cougar."

I was a young girl when Little Fish had nearly drowned as a baby and I rescued him. Now he was all grown up and I was a woman with five children. He kept a soft spot in my heart as he grew up. My heart quivered, knowing that cougars tear their prey to pieces.

"Do you want me to help you?" my John asked Black Whale.

My heart quivered even more, making it hard to breathe. Would my husband and Attitash's put themselves in peril looking for Little Fish?

"Ahhe, I do need your help," Black Whale said.

John's eyebrows went up at that. "What do you need?"

"You to keep eye on Moses Ta-bot." Seeing my John's look, Black Whale continued, "Ta-bot good man. But I be gone nights, not good if your man is alone with our women."

That brought up so many questions that I put my hand over my mouth to keep from spilling them. Did he not trust Moses Talbot? Or Seafoam? Attitash?

John asked nothing. He put his hand out for Black Whale to take. "I trust Talbot," he said. "But I will go to your home, and so will Elisabeth. Attitash will tell her if Talbot is not respectful."

"Catabatash," Black Whale thanked him. He pulled his furs over himself and went out into the storm.

Moses Talbot himself met me at the flap to their hut when I went next to see if he was behaving himself. "I was just going to talk to Howland, Mistress. Does he know Little Fish has not returned from his vision quest? Attitash has such a firm face, I know she's trying to hide her fear for her brother." After I assured him that we knew this, Talbot left to confer with John.

Attitash and Seafoam spilled their fears for Little Fish. Attitash told me a little more of her frightening dream that Black Whale had mentioned. When Seafoam settled down to suckle little Red Berry, I leaned close to Attitash and murmured quickly that Black Whale sought assurance that Moses would not be treating Seafoam rudely while alone.

I rather expected Attitash to laugh at her husband's fears, but she was solemn. "So Jon-owland will remind Ta-bot?"

"Ahhe, he will remind him." Trust comes slowly when we are strangers to each other.

A FEW EVENINGS later, I banked the fires in the common room of our fort. Most of the men had gone to bed, as had Priscilla and John Alden. John and I were gathering our reluctant sleepy children when a banging on the big door to the fort startled us. John opened it a crack, then wider to let Black Whale enter, followed by Little Fish. As they shook snow off and stomped, I filled a kettle and hung it on the fire. I took our three youngest girls upstairs to our rooms and got them settled in their bedding on the floor. When I returned to the common room, John had the fire going again. Some of our men, awakened by the noise, had come down. Black Whale and Little Fish towered over my John and the others.

The water was seething, so I made tea for the frozen visitors. They sat at our table, blowing the hot drink and sipping. All I had to serve them was a slice of left-over cornbread. Little Fish wolfed his down, which made Black Whale laugh. "I have brought my wife's Otter clan brother back from his vision quest. He is no longer a young boy named Little Fish, he is now Fish Hawk. His Clan Uncle, Red Hawk, Seafoam's father, told me before we came here that this would be his new name."

"Fish Hawk," my John repeated. "Seafoam's father is Red Hawk?"

Black Whale nodded. "Red Hawk is Otter Clan—like Attitash and Fish Hawk. He is my wife's brother."

Our son John moved close to Little Fish—now Fish Hawk. I waved him back, but he refused to move. Fish Hawk turned to my boy and said something to him in their language which young John replied to in same. His eyes got big and he turned to me, "Mother, Fish Hawk saw a cougar on his vision quest."

The men stopped talking. I looked at Attitash's brother and husband for confirmation that Attitash's dream she'd told me was true. They nodded in agreement.

"Really? Where was it?" my husband asked.

Fish Hawk drew a deep breath and looked at Black Whale. He said something I thought meant, "Should I tell them? "

"Ahhe, tell." Black Whale replied. Before the story could begin, a flurry at the door brought Attitash. She explained she'd left her children with Seafoam and Talbot so she could visit me too. Everyone crowded together in the common room. Our Desire sat on my lap, though she was so big now we both giggled.

Fish Hawk stood, as a story teller should. His English was better than Black Whale's, but at times he would pause and confer with the others for the right word.

When he got to the part where he heard heavy panting from outside his shelter, none of us took a breath. And when he described looking out next morning and seeing a cougar on top of a boulder close by, Desire put her hand over her mouth.

"I looked at the qumuno—the cougar—and she looked at me," Fish Hawk continued. "I did not feel afraid. The qumuno's face was calm. She did not growl or wave her tail. Her eyes told me she knew me. But I did wonder if I would be able to walk away from there. That night I slept some, but whenever I woke, I could hear the breathing."

His voice was soft but clear. I felt like I was in the heathen shelter covered in snow.

Fish Hawk drew a long breath, as though he were the creature.

"How did you get away?" my son asked when Fish Hawk did not continue.

Fish Hawk laughed quietly. "It was easy. I just waited. Next morning, I woke up and did not hear breathing. I looked carefully outside, she was not there. Nippa'uus was giving a little light and I could see her tracks going away."

"Did you follow them?" little John asked. The men all laughed.

"I am here. I knew I was being allowed to come home." Fish Hawk answered.

7

Elisabeth:

It was late March before the snow began to melt and the streams filled with water. My little Lydia was toddling about. Her hair was as dark as her sister Desire's, making her blue eyes a contrast. Her three big sisters—Desire, Hope, and Elizabeth—took turns holding onto the walking strings to keep Lydia away from the fires. Son John, now eight, stayed close to the Alden boys and ignored all his sisters.

It was still muddy on the trails, but the air was warmer when Seafoam and Attitash brought their babes to visit. They still carried their daughters in cradleboards, though it seemed to me the little girls needed to strengthen their legs. I could not recall how long Attitash kept Mosk in his cradleboard, mayhap I did not notice.

We sat side by side on the bench by our door. Seafoam looked markedly calmer and even smiled at me. I sent my Desire to tell her father we had visitors.

"Will Goodman Talbot want to come, too?" Desire asked. "They are working together splitting wood." She had a pout on her face and I realized that Desire, now ten years old, held hopes that despite their difference in age now, she would interest

Moses when she grew up. She did not realize that Moses Talbot was not only living next door to protect Seafoam but seemed to enjoy the opportunity. That was beyond Desire's ken.

She returned with both her father and Talbot. Desire seemed to notice the smile that lit Moses's face when he saw Seafoam. Seafoam did not return his smile, as she lowered her eyes, but her voice was soft when she greeted him.

As my friends left to find Black Whale, I had to remind Desire to bid them farewell. And remind myself I had to find a time and place to sit down with my daughter. Her gray eyes were showing green. I would have to explain the complicated situation to her.

Attitash:

Black Whale and I knew how to make love silently. However, after a long winter of keeping silent in a crowded wetu with Ta-bot breathing just a few paces away, the warm weather made us eager to express our feelings out loud. Leaving the children with Seafoam, Black Whale and I found a spot similar to our Trees-in-Love back home—branches wrapped around each other. I put all thoughts of restraint out of my mind, joyously crying out. Black Whale did plenty of whoops of his own when he finally gave me his all. We did linger in the silence, the peaceful silence of two lovers happily weary.

When I returned home and took Nipi to suck, Seafoam avoided looking at me. I focused on my baby, milk dripping down my breasts which had filled again as soon as I picked her up. When Nipi popped off and I put her down, Seafoam grabbed my arm. "Why do you get to enjoy your man and I don't?"

Elisabeth:

When the warm nights finally allowed us to open the shutter, the moonlight fell on our bed and I could at last see John's face when he leaned over me. I traced his mouth, his cheeks, and felt his hair. We often followed our lovemaking with quiet talk, but that night I was so sated that I snuggled in to sleep against his shoulder.

"Are ye sleepy, Love?" Eyes closed, I murmured in assent, but my husband continued, "Talbot came and talked to me today."

I hoped my husband was not going to tell me that Moses Talbot realized our young daughter had eyes for him. I had not had the talk with Desire yet, what with her younger sisters always close to hand. Forcing my eyes open, I whispered, "Did he say something ye want to talk about now?"

John laughed softly. "Not at length." He pulled up the light blanket against the night air. "He says it's time for him to become Seafoam's husband."

Now I was awake. "What did ye tell Moses?"

John shifted so he could see my face in the dim moonlight. "I told him to talk to Black Whale. If he agrees, then go slow. Ask Seafoam to marry and then be discreet."

John's words jumped way ahead of my thoughts—wouldn't Attitash and Seafoam be the ones to give permission? What would "marry" mean if a Christian married a heathen? And discretion was only possible in the forest. I remembered the first time lying with John behind the bed curtains in Brewsters' household when we bundled. "What do you mean, 'be discreet?' No one could be discreet in a crowded little hut."

"I mean he must never touch her in public—outside their home."

Attitash:

When Seafoam asked, "Why do you get to enjoy your man and I don't," I wondered if she was thinking of Ta-bot or might be wanting now to be Black Whale's second wife. I tried not to let the disturbance in my belly show in my face.

My response, "Which man do you expect to enjoy?" was

met with a blank look. Seafoam turned away, her shoulders slumping.

Nipi wanted out of her cradleboard and I was distracted by tending to her. I wished I were back home with my family in our own village. Living with the Abenaki so far from home was lonely and facing all this trouble with Seafoam was wearing me down.

The next few days, however, I noticed that Moses Ta-bot seemed to be moving into Seafoam's space—standing closer when he spoke to her, touching her shoulder, her arm, laughing with her as if at some secret joke. He acted like our men do when they want a woman. But maybe the Strangers moved close to women without signaling anything. I repeated her words in my head and saw that she must now consider Moses Ta-bot her man. And she wanted to enjoy him. I finally asked her directly, "Do you want Ta-bot as a husband now?"

Seafoam could not hide her big smile. "He asked me last night to join our circles."

Both relief and dread filled my heart. Black Whale would remain mine alone. But the possibilities for my cousin's betrayal by a Stranger were unsettling. "And you said yes?"

"I didn't say yes, but I didn't say no." Seafoam took my hand. "Dear Attitash. You need not warn me. I said yes to Shimmering Fish, then suffered as his wife." She bit her lip, tears slid from the corners of her eyes. "I took the Narragansett because I had to." Seafoam drew a deep breath, squeezing my hand. "And I said NO to Pit-Face, but suffered terribly anyway."

"Are you afraid to refuse Ta-bot?"

"No," Seafoam smiled again. "He's gentle. I just don't think I can easily or quickly be a wife again."

"So what did you say?"

"I said, 'Give me time. Go slow.'"

They did go slow. One evening, when the small rivers filled the Kennebec, Ta-bot sat close and put his arm around

Seafoam as we sat by the fire. Black Whale was obviously glancing at them frequently but said nothing.

Next day, my husband found me hoeing the little plot we'd been given. "Ta-bot wants Seafoam to pray for healing with him to his god."

"Where did you hear this?"

"He told me himself this morning. Says he wants his god to make sure she's healed before she agrees to mate."

I had no response for this until I'd talked to Seafoam. I caught up with her as she repacked Red Berry's cradleboard with fresh cat-tail fluff.

"What could it hurt?" she asked when I reminded her that she'd already received healing from our spirits. "If it makes Moses believe I'm ready for him, that's good."

"Are you?"

Seafoam bit her lip. "It has been a long time since I wanted to join. But I think I do now."

After supper that night Jon-owland and Esapett came to our fire. Moses Ta-bot and Seafoam sat together while Jon-owland and Esapett raised their hands and spoke with strong voices. They asked their god to "Shed Seafoam's memory of the sin and give her grace. Help her to forgive the one who sinned against her."

I did not understand their words, "grace" and "sin." I remembered hearing about 'giving-for,' but the words made no sense. Ta-bot looked happy. However, Seafoam seemed confused by their words and actions—no doubt expecting a soothing chanting of prayers instead. When Esapett and Jon-owland began to sing, although their voices stayed mostly on the same droning level, Seafoam's face softened and her stiff shoulders relaxed. When our friends had finished their words and singing, Black Whale made two birch half-hoops. He gave one to Moses and the other to Seafoam. Then they put the two halves together and lashed them to make one hoop. We all sang a joining song for Seafoam and Ta-bot.

When dark came and we went into our little wetu, Black Whale put an arm on Ta-bot. "It takes time, even if the gods hear you. Stay away from Seafoam tonight."

Moses Ta-bot nodded, his face set in determination. He touched Seafoam tenderly on her shoulder, then went to his own place on the sleeping bench.

The next night, Ta-bot went again to his place. Seafoam snuggled with her baby, singing Red Berry to sleep. Our Mosk and little Nipi quickly dropped into deep sleep, too. Black Whale was quietly nuzzling my neck when Seafoam put her sleeping baby next to my Nipi, then without a word moved to where Moses Ta-bot lay. They were quiet, but not silent. I heard hushed moans, giggles, heavy sighs and sometimes outright laughter.

8

Elisabeth:

"Is my son John with your son?"

In the two years since we'd moved to the Koussinoc, Priscilla and I had become accustomed to the tall, dense forests, the big Kennebec River, and the proximity of the Abenaki people. But our two sons were too young to believe there were also dangers.

Priscilla glanced about the open area surrounding the fort, and seeing no boys, called to our oldest daughters, "Elizabeth! Desire! Where are thy brothers?"

Our girls, sitting on a bench plaiting each other's hair, shrugged their shoulders. "Nay worry. Those boys are too wild to tempt the bears," my Desire laughed.

Elizabeth Alden joined in the giggling. "Ooh, what a bad tasting dish."

Priscilla made a face at her Elizabeth. "Don't try to be witty about thy brother, Daughter."

The brother himself appeared, Priscilla's young John Alden, dark eyes like his father and fair hair like hers. My son John was the same age. At eight, they were a year past being forgiven for childish mischief. But now they were too animated to pay attention to an older sister's chiding. "Mother," my son called. "Runners from the Abenaki sent word to Father that a new barq is coming up-river."

"From near the sea, a day away," his friend added.

"Do they know who's coming?" Priscilla and I asked simultaneously. A barq was a vessel similar to our shallop, any Christian might be in such a boat.

"Father says that it could be the Boston men," young John said.

"Hocking?" I asked under my breath, but my son's ears picked up everything.

"I asked Father." John shook his brown hair out of his face. He was still quite disheveled from running, but at least I could see his eyes. "He said he couldn't rule it out." With that, the boys took off again.

"Where are Attitash and Seafoam?" I asked my daughter.

Desire shrugged her shoulders. "I saw them early on, going into the woods to collect plants for remedies."

Priscilla kept her head down, looking at her hands as if she held a secret in them. When she lifted her light blue eyes to me, they were guarded. "Have John Howland and ye thought how long ye intend to keep the Plimoth Indians here at the trading post?"

"Why would they leave before we do?" In fact, we had not spoken at all of Attitash and Black Whale going back to Plimoth—nor of Seafoam. We did speak nearly every day of when we could take our family and return to Plimoth. The answer from my John was always, "When everything is settled with the treaty rights."

Now I looked at my friend, who for so many years had tolerated Attitash, but seldom spoke to her. Priscilla had come from a family with servants. They had died along with her parents and her brother that first winter. I didn't remember much about how she'd treated her servants, but it must have been similar to her attitude with Attitash and Black Whale.

"If Seafoam's presence threatens the rest of us, it might be time for her to leave." Priscilla looked away from me, towards where the Kennebec River flowed to the sea.

I studied Priscilla to ascertain whether she was serious or jesting. Her face was set, her mouth a straight line. Fear glinted in her eyes. Priscilla's hands clenched tightly in a fist. "Surely thy husband has told thee that the poacher got Seafoam with child—her bastard."

My own hands made a fist. "Yea, I know that—a forced mating which caused Seafoam to flee and almost die alone in the great forest." It irked me that my old friend thought she might know something I'd not been told. I tried to compose my face so Priscilla would not notice I was hiding my own fear. Truth be told, John and I had in fact discussed that very possibility Priscilla alluded to—an act of revenge by Hocking. But my husband had insisted we were secure and Hocking would not dare to invade our place at the trading fort. "The less said the better," my John had warned me. "Do not be part of gossip which spreads fear."

I concluded my best response was to draw out her fear rather than fan its flame.

"Why does Seafoam's suffering make thee afraid, Priscilla? She is rid of Hocking. Furthermore, Moses Talbot is protecting her." I turned my head toward the Kennebec and then looked about our trading post. "No boat, shallop or barq, can come up-river without our knowing. Our men—your John and mine as well as their company here—are well armed."

Priscilla sighed heavily. "Ye were just thirteen, a child really, that terrible first winter when we lost our parents and so many others. I am just enough older than ye to remember when our men were attacked by the savages." Priscilla rubbed her arms as if to shed a foul covering. "Mayhap ye did not understand how quickly trouble stirs up. Even if we can defend against poachers, the Abenaki savages here and thy

Wampanoag friends could decide to join forces against us."

I was at a loss for words. All these years—fourteen—since that dreadful first winter, and now my old friend was re-living that harrowing time. "Of course, I remember," I told Priscilla. She was the only woman friend of my own kind here at the trading post. I did not want to admonish her, nor did I want her fears to inflame the rest of our little settlement and lead to sending Attitash and Black Whale away. Not only did I like having Attitash near, we needed them to negotiate with the Abenaki. Priscilla's life had been upended years ago when her high status became lower than mine. When Plimoth was organized into companies to strengthen our defense, John Alden was listed in John Howland's company. Later, after cattle were brought over and we all made profit with them, John Alden and Priscilla built a real house on property just north of Plimoth. John and Priscilla became settled landowners, but he still was in the company led by my husband when we came to the Koussinoc Trading Post. My John conferred with John Alden and the other men in his company, but he made the ultimate decisions.

"We shall ask my husband about this when he and your John return, Priscilla," I assured her. "If ye reveal thy fears to them, we can find out what is planned."

That evening, before I even broached the subject, Priscilla, in her high-pitched lady's voice, put the question to my John. "What does our esteemed captain plan to do in order to reduce the threat to us Christians created by the heathen girl's presence?"

John Alden spoke up before my John could respond. "Prissy asked a question; she must need an answer. We've had enough of Rutting Girl and the trouble she brings. Send the savages back to their king Massasowet."

"I am not convinced we would be safer without Black Whale and his family," my husband replied. "We need his skill with the bow and arrow, and his translations."

John Alden flushed. He must have expected a more positive rejoinder. "Then at least send away the slut Moses Talbot consorts with."

"Seafoam is not a slut," I said, without concern for offending John Alden or Priscilla. "Talbot and Seafoam were married in an Indian ceremony."

I knew John Alden did not believe one could "marry" a savage, but I hoped Priscilla would understand. It was possible that my defense of Seafoam would damage my friendship with Priscilla, leaving me without a close friend of my own kind while we were in Maine. However, if I held my tongue, Attitash and her entire family would suffer from the accusations against Seafoam. Priscilla and John looked at my husband—if he sided with me, they would have to choose whether to stand their ground or succumb to their leader's position.

My John was not looking at any of us. He was cleaning his knife, rubbing it over and over with sand, then a greased rag. He finally looked up. "I shall consider thy advice, Alden. We must not forget our safety, as ye said, but also not be too hasty in our decision."

Our friends looked disappointed but did not argue.

When we were alone, I turned on John "We must find a way out of this morass without inflicting pain on Attitash and Black Whale!" He put his arm around me, stroking my hair.

"Yea, we must, and we will. But our friends need to discover this slowly."

THINGS WENT BADLY AWRY next morning. Priscilla and I were heating water for washing when our servant boy, William Latham, came running from the river, holding both of our young boys by the arms.

"Poachers coming up-river!" William shouted. "Keep the boys here." My composure crumpled and my hands fluttered as I tried to think.

William shoved the boys to us and turned to go back. I grabbed my son by the neck and shouted at young Latham, "Wait, William, what's going on?"

The boy heard the 'mistress' in my voice and stopped. "Master Howland is taking his men in a longboat to chase the poachers out." William glanced back to shore. "Master Howland might need more ammunition. Bring some."

If John was in danger from poachers, I had to get to the river immediately. But he'd also asked for more gun shot, so I tried to slow my heart and calm my hands. I grabbed the bandoliers filled with shot and flung them over my shoulder. Fighting to keep the tension from pitching my voice high, I commanded my daughter, "Keep everyone in the house, Desire. No matter what ye hear."

Priscilla and I hitched our skirts high so we could run. We caught sight of Attitash and Seafoam ahead of us, running to the river.

Attitash:

As I arrived at the river, a shot exploded across the water. I saw a man in Jon-owland's canoe slump. I dropped to the ground. My body burned with the memory of gunfire in my body—as fresh as the day I was shot. Another shot rang out. Peering through the bush, I saw a man on the bigger wind-canoe fall back. Frantically, I looked for Black Whale and my brother who'd gone ahead of us. Would my man have taken the dugout canoe into the river? But there was no sign of a dark man with feathers in his topknot.

Elisabeth:

A crack like thunder shattered the air, followed quickly by more. My bones melted and my legs went out from under me. I gulped air and forced my body up, creeping toward the shore. As we came in view of the Kennebec River, I saw a barq near our longboat. It had to be from the Boston gentry—sending poachers to invade our territory and take our beaver from the Abenaki.

Shouts came across the water. As we reached the banks and could see better, I tried to distinguish John amidst the men in the boats. Attitash and Seafoam were crawling out from bushes near the beach. They must have seen what happened when the guns were fired. A sick feeling of helpless fear gripped me.

"I brought bandoliers," I called, futilely, holding them high. No one could hear me over the tumbling river. I stood, arms hanging and shoulders sagging. Realizing I could be a target myself, I dropped down on my haunches.

Men in both boats leaned over something—someone? I tried to scream, "Is someone shot?" But my heart thumping against my ribs took my breath and turned my words into an anguished whisper.

Attitash came back toward me, trying to get me to understand her over the chaotic sounds of shouting and the river pouring over rocks. She lurched forward. I caught her and almost fell myself. "Men shot dead," she blurted out.

I froze. I could not speak nor move. I knew I should check Attitash for injury, but my arms would not obey my thoughts.

Seafoam stood in the river, screaming at the boat. Attitash stood mute in front of me. Breathing was nigh impossible. Like I was under water. Gun smoke drifted toward shore. As the wind caught the gray haze, it cleared our view. I searched the scene, hoping for sight of my John. When a man with dark hair showing beneath his beaver hat sat up and turned toward me, air rushed into my body. Surely that was my husband. As the longboat came closer, I sobbed with relief to see my beloved's face.

When the boat hit shore, I could see someone, held by another man, with blood running from his throat and covering his chest. His head of blond hair stained bright red hung back uselessly. Moses Talbot! Was he still alive?

Attitash:

A gray-faced Stranger lay in another man's arms on the bottom of the canoe. Yellow hair fell in bloody clumps on his red-stained face. Moses Ta-bot! Jon-owland and others lifted Ta-bot's body out and laid him on the sand.

Seafoam's shrill voice tore the air. My cousin flung herself on Ta-bot. I moved toward her slowly, knowing she was too distraught to be taken away yet. I sat with her, my arms across her back as she sobbed convulsively. All other sound stopped for me. No birds shrieking. Not even the Kennebec River dashing against the rocky shore got through to my ears.

Elisabeth:

Seafoam's "Áieeee" turned to a howl that curdled every drop of blood in my body. She clung to Moses' body. Talbot's face was gray his body limp. John's dear face was pale as candle wax and rigid, as he spoke urgently to the other men. My husband went to pick Seafoam up, but she clung to the bloody corpse. John stepped back and at last spoke to me.

"Moses is dead. The murderous man who killed him is too."

I went to him and put my arms around him. It was like embracing a stone. I waited until my husband at last raised his head from my embrace and took both my hands.

"It's all gone wrong, Elisabeth." His words came out in gasps. I held my tongue as he fought to gain control. "This should not have been done. Not to Moses."

"Who killed him?"

"Hocking." John spat the word out. "Now Hocking's dead. He brought it on himself."

I waited for my husband to tell me how Hocking had died.

"God help us," was all John said. He started to turn back to his men who were ready to carry home Talbot's body, but noticing my face, he paused. "We'll talk later. Go home to make sure the children are safe."

Attitash:

My eyes scoured the woods for Black Whale and Fish Hawk until finally I could see them coming from the woods. Black Whale came to me, his eyes burning with anguish. "Tell Esapett to watch for Fish Hawk. He has something for her from me." I thought it might be the firestick—the gun—Jon-owl-and had given him. He looked back at my brother, who stood waiting at the edge of the woods, then turned to me

"I will take Seafoam back home." Black Whale picked her up and slowly walked up the path. He held her careful-ly, almost tenderly. She leaned her head into his shoulder as though she were already a sister-wife. My throat ached. Sea-foam would need Black Whale now. I would have to share my husband.

"The children are in our wetu," I called to Black Whale. I turned back to look for Fish Hawk and saw him approaching Esapett.

Elisabeth:

Priscilla stood watching the scene, wringing her hands. "This is what we hoped to avoid!"

"Dear friend," I said to her as calmly as I could manage. "Could ye go stay with our children? They'll have heard shots and be terrified. I'll come as soon as I find out what's happening."

Priscilla cast her bright blue eyes at me. "Oh yea, with all this trouble I near forgot our little ones!"

I saw Fish Hawk motion to me. I could still remember when he was Little Fish, a wiggling babe whom I'd rescued from a swift stream thirteen years ago. Now a man with an adult name, he was even taller than Black Whale.

John and the other men were struggling to carry the body up the bank. Fish Hawk stopped about ten paces from me and, checking about to make sure no one was watching, carefully put down a small bundle wrapped in leather. Fish Hawk brushed sand over it, then picked up a few shells—as if that were why he was kneeling on the sand. Without looking at me, Fish Hawk spoke in a low, but distinct voice. "When others can no longer see or hear you, take this back to your house."

I kept my eyes on the river and my voice as low as Fish Hawk's. "Is this something Black Whale no longer wants?"

"Ahhe." He stood up. The danger we were all in now hit me in my gut. It was illegal in Plimoth and Boston for Indians to possess guns. But when we moved to the trading post, my John had given Black Whale one of his own pistols, saying that Black Whale might need it if we were attacked. No one here at Koussinoc could tell John what to do. But now, two men had been shot. If Black Whale or Fish Hawk were caught with a gun, they would be hanged. And if John was found to have given the pistol to a savage, he might be too.

Fish Hawk moved off without looking at me. When he was out of view, I walked with heavy legs to where he'd buried the object. If anyone knew what it was, I would be asked questions I could not answer. I knelt down and scooped the sand away until the bundle was exposed. Taking off my apron, I looked to the river. The barq was long gone. No one was in view on shore either. I quickly wrapped the heavy bundle with my apron. When I reached my garden, I hid the bundle under my wash tub. I would wait until dark and John was home to move it to a safe place.

Returning to my room, I found Priscilla had told her five children and mine that someone had died. Every last one of them was giddy with fright. Desire and Elizabeth Alden were too distraught to keep the little ones quiet.

"Everyone line up," Priscilla ordered. "Howlands by the bed and Aldens across from them!" She may not have been perfect with our Indian friends, but Priscilla knew how to get servants and children organized. With relief that my own family was unharmed, I looked at my five children lined up by age: Desire, John, Hope, Elizabeth, and little Lydia.

"What's happening? Where is Father?" Their questions boiled over.

"Thy fathers will tell thee when they get here." Priscilla replied. Her children looked submissive, but mine continued to blurt out queries.

"Truth be told," I said, after I'd threatened the rod to make them quiet, "There were poachers on the river, but…" I silenced their words with a stern look. "Moses Talbot was shot." The children cried out in one shocked voice. "But thank the Lord, thy fathers are both safe," I continued. "The poacher who killed Goodman Talbot was killed. They fled down river."

"Not Goodman Talbot!" my young John cried. "Who shot his murderer?"

"Father will tell thee after he returns," I told my son.

"They'll find out soon enough," I murmured to Priscilla whose face was contorted with the need to avoid the issue until their fathers were with them.

The children knew there would be no more answers. My Desire was fighting to hold in her tears. "I think I'm sick," she blurted and headed for the door. I followed her outside and held her hair back while she puked onto the muck heap. Moses had been a man she could imagine loving. When she was emptied out, I gave her a dipper of water. She drank quickly and I took her in my arms to bury her cries. I felt my own heart wail with hers, though I kept my cries inside.

Priscilla and I agreed that she and her children would stay with me in our rooms until our husbands returned. It felt too lonely, if not too dangerous, for us to be alone. We set about getting them fed, but both of us were cross with the boys and short-tempered with even the little ones. After feeding them supper, we put them all to sleep together on my floor. The little children cuddled up together like a litter of puppies. My Desire lay with closed eyes, but her face was taut for a long time.

THE NEW MOON SHOWN in the west when our men at last returned home. My John was as grim-faced as John Alden. Without a word to either of us, her John helped Priscilla carry their children back to their rooms. Priscilla had said nothing during all this time about Seafoam causing the tragedy, but I was relieved when she left. Surely, she and John Alden understood now that it was not Seafoam, but the bounty of furs and timber, that drew Hocking and his henchmen?

My husband took a long draft of ale, then pulled me close. "Moses is buried. Hocking is dead." He said, as if he'd forgotten he'd already told me.

I bit my tongue to hold back all my questions. Who killed Hocking? Were we safer now? Or would his crew retaliate?

I left his embrace and went down to the garden to bring the pistol from its hiding place. I gave the bundle, still wrapped in my apron, to John. As soon as he took it from my hands, his puzzled expression changed to anxiety. As he unwrapped the pistol, his eyebrows lifted in shock.

"It's the one I gave Black Whale. Who gave it to thee?"

I briefly told him of the covert exchange. He checked the pistol, shaking out the remains of black powder, then put it with his other guns on the weapon-hooks high up. We were both silent for a long time, then I had to ask, "Can ye tell me what happened?"

He leaned his forehead against mine and let out a long breath. "Nay, I cannot."

I waited a few beats. We'd long ago agreed that he would tell me only what he could, but that he would never lie. "Why not?"

He lifted his head and traced the curve of my cheek with his hand. "I don't know if I understand what happened." Taking both my hands, John held them so tight it almost hurt. "Hocking may have known Seafoam was living with Moses Talbot. Or he may have just been trying to steal all the bounty the Abenaki brought to us at the trading post." John released my hands and soothed me by patting my back. "Hocking had anchored his barq. I told our men to cut the cable—send him back downriver. But before it was cut, Hocking drew near our boat and pulled out his pistol. I called out, 'If you're going to shoot someone, shoot me. I'm the one in charge.'"

Sobs shook him and as he pulled me close, his silent sobs convulsed me too. Our bodies trembled together. "Then a gun went off and Moses went down."

"And they got away after he killed Moses?"

"Well, the cable released, so their barq started to drift. But Hocking was down by then."

"Do ye know who killed Hocking?" I wanted to call back my question, seeing the agony in John's face. It was the same expression he'd had after Attitash was shot when we were young.

John clasped my hands again. "Someone killed Hocking and if the Boston Lords find out, someone good will be hanged for the likes of Hocking."

"Did more than one man shoot his gun?" I could not voice my question—would it be my husband?

The anguish on John's face told me his own fear. "Yea. More than one shot. We may spend the rest of our lives sorting this out."

9

Attitash:

If Seafoam slept, I only knew this because her sobs stopped. I held her in my arms, hoping her trembling would ease. Black Whale and my brother rose early, took little Mosk with them and left for the weir. Seafoam's daughter, Red Berry, slept with my Nipi. When the girls woke, Red Berry toddled over, looking for her mother. Not wanting her to wake Seafoam, I gave the child my own teat. After I settled Red Berry in her cradleboard, I suckled my Nipi and made my plan. Seafoam would have to go back home to her mother. I could not heal her alone. But how she would get there, I could not imagine yet.

Elisabeth:

John and I slept tangled up but did not speak or kiss. When I dozed, I jerked awake from a dream of struggles under water as the limp body of Moses Talbot spilled blood that stained the depths around me. The dream would not fade. I lay next to my beloved husband, all my muscles cramped. To push away the image of Moses bloodied and weak, I brought back the memory of Moses alive—his strong arms lifting up

Seafoam's baby, his strong hands touching mine briefly. Sobs shook me and woke John. He gently pulled me close, then his own sobs joined mine. We clung to each other until our weeping was spent at last.

When I rose at dawn, my mind was as slow as ice melting in midwinter. My hands did what they needed to do, but they were not connected to my brain. One foot after the other to get out of bed. Stumble to the muck heap to lift my night shift and relieve myself. Get my son to bring water from the spring. The children were quarreling with each other but I paid no attention. John sat staring into space long after he'd finished his meager break-fast.

William Latham approached John, looking haggard. He'd probably not slept either. Moses had taken William under his wing and the young man was no doubt now realizing his loss. "Master, the men are awaiting you at the river. The Abenaki have a fresh lot of fish from their weir to be sorted and reckoned." As John left, he touched my shoulder in passing, a tentative gesture which moved me by its restraint.

Later, I would think back to the sudden turn in our lives that morning.

"AIEEE, SEAFOAM IS GONE!" Attitash's distress call was shrill. I could not understand all her words. However, I could hear the fear and ran to her hut.

I found Attitash outside, calling for Seafoam. "Have you seen her anywhere?" Attitash asked me. "She wouldn't go far without her daughter."

Hopeless as it might be, we searched for Seafoam on the shore. But so many footprints crossed each other in the sand there was no possibility of following Seafoam's.

When the men arrived home for dinner, they joined our search. All afternoon we called while following the trails through the woods, led by Black Whale, Fish Hawk, and Attitash. She let my Desire carry little Red Berry, since we mothers both had a babe two years old ourselves to manage.

As the sun settled behind the northern hills, we Christians gathered in prayer. My heart told me it was useless to hunt for Seafoam. The woman was so hysterical over Moses' death that she'd left her little daughter behind. If Seafoam had not had so much tragedy—with her first husband, Shimmering Fish, then a Narragansett husband, then Hocking—mayhap she could have endured Moses's murder. My thoughts scattered and instead of praying for Seafoam, I prayed for my husband. A chill gripped my ribs as I realized Hocking's men would no doubt implicate my John. They could accuse my husband of murder and call for his hanging. We had all been present for John Billington's hanging, though I confess I did not look, and did not carry the grim vision in my mind's eye. Being present, with eyes closed, was dreadful enough. A jury of twelve men had found Billington guilty. But here at the Koussinoc Trading Post we had no court, no jury to hear our side of the story. My desperation shook my hands, uplifted in prayer. If my John were...

But I could not let even God hear that thought. God would not let my beloved swing from a broken neck.

Attitash:

When Nippa'uus disappeared over the western hills, the Strangers met to talk to their gods and we went to the Abenaki village. The Abenaki women promised to look for signs of Seafoam. One young girl thought that as she looked for clams, she'd heard something splashing in the river, but wasn't sure if it was a fish, a river otter, or a person.

Black Whale and Fish Hawk talked with the Abenaki warriors, hoping they'd seen or heard something of our lost loved one. Black Whale reported that no one had seen or heard anything, but they promised to watch for signs as they checked their traps.

"Did you talk with the Abenaki about the deaths on the water?" I asked.

"Only that the Strangers were fighting with each other and one was killed from each canoe."

His answer was too short. I wondered if any Abenaki knew my husband had a firestick. Was it possible my husband had used the pistol against the man who killed Moses Talbot? I pushed the thoughts down. My husband could tell me when we were alone.

When we brought Seafoam's little Red Berry to the Abenaki Grandmothers' Caucus to heal, the oldest grandmother held Red Berry. "We can help heal this child, but we may not be able to find her mother," the grandmother said. She blew sweet grass smoke on Red Berry to call all the spirits, then wafted sage smoke in her face to send away the bad spirits. The child watched her with big eyes, then let dreams gather her spirit to slumber.

I softly sang, "Rockabye, Baby, in the tree top, when the wind blows, the cradleboard rocks," to keep her sleeping. The grandmothers anointed her with healing water.

I did not want to go home and try to sleep; but there would be no chance of finding Seafoam after dark. If only I had been able to take Seafoam to our Wampanoag grandmothers before she disappeared. They tried to teach Seafoam, not shun her as these Abenaki grandmothers did. Our Wampanoag grandmothers would have healed her. But I had not and now Seafoam was missing. I did not want to go home without her, but there would be no chance of finding anyone after dark. We would have to find Seafoam in the morning.

Black Whale and Fish Hawk were silent as we brought the children back to our wetu. As we walked through the dark path, it seemed as though Seafoam would call out to us suddenly. But the only sound was tree branches scraping in the wind.

When we were back home, I put the two little girls with

me on the sleeping bench. Black Whale looked at them, cuddled into each other. He did not ask me to leave them and sleep with him. I was both relieved and disappointed. My feelings were as raw as if I had been scraping them with my deerskin-smoothing stick.

Elisabeth:

We fell asleep as soon as we had all the children settled. It was long into the night when I woke to find John moaning in his sleep and trembling. He lay with his back to me. Was he dreaming, as I had, about encountering Moses's body underwater? My attempt to wake him gently by stroking his back worked, in so far as his trembling stopped and he was quiet. He sat up and shrugged his shoulders back and forth. I put my head close against him to hear, as he spoke in a low voice.

"I knew it would be dangerous, but this was not supposed to happen." He turned to me. I could hardly see his face but heard the agony in his voice. "Not to Moses. Not to anyone."

I had no answer, just leaned in close and slid my arms beneath his. He embraced me with such fierceness that I struggled to catch my breath. Without another word he began stroking me, touching me everywhere—with his hands, his tongue, his arms. His ardor was not tender. It was rage, strength, power. When he entered me, I almost succumbed to passive acceptance, but my fears and anguish provided me the strength to wrap my legs around him, grasp his back and hang on. When we were both spent and lay together, tears covered my face and I could not distinguish mine from John's.

He buried his face in my shoulder. "I'm sorry I couldn't save Moses."

"We are all sorry," I whispered back. "Hocking deserved to die."

"Yea, he did." John went silent. His breathing was still

labored, so I knew he was struggling with his emotions. "And Moses did not. But I hope it doesn't take a court to decide that."

"What court? We don't have one here."

"Ye know that the men in the barq have gone back to Boston. They no doubt will tell their story to the Boston financiers and write to their lordships in England."

I knew there were wealthy gentry who were never satisfied, always wanting more, but I'd never met any lords. Many tales were told of how they now tried to rule in Boston as well as back home. "What lordships?"

"Lord Say and Lord Brooke. Since we came up here, they have financed the plantation on the Piscataqua River in New Hampshire." Having finished his sparse tale, John turned over and fell back asleep.

I lay breathing. One breath in. Another breath out. Not asking who killed Hocking.

Attitash:

"I dreamed about Seafoam." Black Whale lay with his back to me. I had just opened my eyes and thought he was still asleep until he spoke. His words were soft and my heart clenched, thinking he'd had a tender dream about the missing Seafoam. Black Whale turned over to face me. Still whispering, "She's gone, Attitash."

"Of course she's gone. We've been looking for her." I could hear Seafoam's little daughter babbling with Nipi. They would want to get up soon. I sat up and looked at Black Whale. He did not look at me, but pulled me back to lie with him, our faces close together.

"I had a dream. We were in the river—you and I and the children—close to shore, splashing and laughing. Then something bumped my leg." His arms tightened around me.

"It was Seafoam."

"Was she swimming?" My breath came hard. I forced a deep one.

"She was not. She had left her body for the Spirit World. It was just Seafoam's body, floating in the river. Then I saw Moses Ta-bot's body, floating next to Seafoam's."

My words burst from my throat without thinking. "Black Whale, who killed the man who shot Moses?"

Black Whale sat up, his face turned to the children, who were chattering with each other. I moved closer to him. Finally, he took my hand and looked deep into my eyes. "Jon-owland says he doesn't know. It was too confusing, lots of shots at close range."

"Did you have Jon-owland's pistol with you?" I had to ask. My husband was a strong warrior. I knew he would gladly kill any Stranger who came to murder our friends. But he only killed with his club or bow and arrow. If my beloved would be taken prisoner by Strangers because he carried a gun, even if he had not killed the poacher, he would be hanged.

"I did shoot." Black Whale gripped my hand harder. "But I was on shore—I don't know if my fire could reach. Jon-owland and his men were right there in the other boat." Black Whale released my hand and rubbed his eyes. "But I used the gun. If anyone finds out, the Strangers could tie me to a tree and leave me to die."

I took both his hands, pressing them to my heart. "The Strangers—even our friends, Esapett and Jon-owland—must never know. We will never speak of Jon-owland's pistols or any other firestick again."

Black Whale returned the strength of my hands with his. "Ahhe, it must be a silent memory."

"Cleanse your hands of all traces of Jon-owland's gun," I told him.

Black Whale spat on his hands and rubbed them. I reached for my herb pouch hanging over our sleeping bench and brought some fragrant mint leaves. He held out his palms and I rubbed them with the leaves.

The little girls began to whine, wanting out of their cradleboards, wanting food. As I started to swing my legs over the edge of the sleeping bed, Black Whale put a hand on my shoulder. "We have to leave."

"Do you mean we need to go back home? Can we?" My heart lifted to think I would see Mama, Papa, and my sister, White Flower.

"I will tell Jon-owland we start the journey back home tomorrow. He will understand how dangerous it is for us— and for him—if we stay here." Black Whale stood up and pulled me with him. "When the Strangers who killed Ta-bot get back to Boston, they will send men here for revenge. We cannot be here. The bad Strangers come to destroy us. They want all the fur and they know we help our friends here."

I lay awake, my arm resting on his chest, feeling his breath rise and fall. It would be a long journey home. But we would be home. We would tell my Clan Uncle Red Hawk and Aunt First Star that their daughter had gone to the spirit world. We could pretend we thought Seafoam had gone somewhere else, but that would only delay their grief. Aunt First Star would take Red Berry into their Beaver clan. Our Wampanoag people would accept Red Berry's curly light hair and light brown face. Mama and Papa would see their granddaughter, Nipi, for the first time. Nipi and Mosk would be home with our Otter clan.

Elisabeth:

Attitash came early in the morning, her back bent from the little girls' cradleboards.

"We must go back home." Tears welled in her eyes.

I felt both a deep sadness and relief. It would be dangerous for my friends to stay with us—both for them and for us. Attitash and Black Whale were like milk in the pail to greedy flies, tempting the lords to come drive out what they considered savages who threatened their ambitions to take over the whole of the fur trade.

Attitash and I had not said goodbye for two years. In Plimoth, she always went with her family back to their main village during the winter, and returned again when the ice melted. Now, she would leave soon and if we saw each other again, it would be when John and I also returned to Plimoth.

Later, when John came home for noon dinner, I told him of Black Whale, Attitash, and Fish Hawk going home and asked when we might go back as well.

"We can't go home to Plimoth now," John said abruptly. "We are in the middle of trading season. All the Abenaki are starting to arrive with the beaver skins trapped during the winter. The ships will be in Boston now, with more supplies to trade. Someone will have to go there to bring back the goods."

"I wish we could just go home to Plimoth and forget the trade." I had helped every year with the inventory of goods shipped from England. There were items for our own use—shot, powder and guns—and items we needed for trading for the furs—cloth, thread, nails, hatchets, iron pots and blankets.

John took the bowl of fish chowder I'd dished up for him. Our children sat on the bed, waiting for their father to finish and invite them to eat. "I'm not the man to go this year. I must be here to defend our treaty and this fort if the Boston Lords who sent Hocking here seek revenge."

"Revenge?" My belly clenched, pulling my navel as if a hidden string was in my body "How could their lordships know what would happen up here on the Kennebec?"

John did not seem to notice the fear in my voice, making it sound like a child's. He nodded to the children to come eat, then sat back and wiped his mouth. "Hocking's men got away immediately, a swift downstream current carrying them to the mouth of the Kennebec. With Hocking's body in their barq, they probably buried him at sea with little ceremony and fled to Boston. We have no way of finding out what tale has gone ahead of us."

"But the gentry in Boston and those in England who sent Hocking to our territory will have heard just one side of the Hocking story." None of this made sense to me. Yet the fear gripping my body would not let me assume anything was sensible.

"Any revenge would be based on ignorance of the facts. Don't the Boston Lords take orders from King James?"

"Yea, remember our trade treaty is from the King. But the Lords in England will only know what they read in the first letter that reaches them. Hocking's men will be sending a letter on the next boat from Boston—which could be within a week. The financiers, Lord Brooke and Lord Say will tell that version to the King." My husband's mouth pursed as though he'd just taken a bite of cranberry without maple syrup to sweeten. "Boston men could accuse us of murder and send militia here. If I'm not here to defend our goods and people, with the King's consent they would take over all our beaver, moose, fox, otter, and other fur trade."

My fears were usually eased when John took the time to explain things to me. Not this time. I ran his words back and forth in my mind. The treaty with the Abenaki was made in 1630. It gave us trade fifteen miles down from the Kennebec waterfall. How could King James let that treaty be abused? In the past fourteen years, as I became a married woman and mother of children, John told me much about this burden of paying off the gentry financiers in England. In the safe confines of our home in Plimoth, it never troubled me. So far, our treaties had worked out just fine. It was paying off the financiers that caused trouble. Trouble? Not compared to my husband being jailed or even hanged for murder. Trouble was hardly the word for murders. Terror was more like it.

I fought back the dizzy feeling in my head that came with

understanding that the world I'd lived with half my life could come crashing down.

John stood up to return to work. I had more questions, however, and put a hand on his arm. I understood now that someone had to go to Boston to get supplies.

"If ye can't go, who will?"

"John Alden will go. He was not with us when the shooting occurred. The Boston leaders can't accuse him of the shooting. Alden should be able to convince them it was self-defense."

A thought stuck to my mind, like a sliver under my finger. John Alden held little if any respect for Black Whale and Attitash. Would his efforts to prove my husband's innocence taint Black Whale and Attitash? I would not reveal this concern out loud, but John took notice of the fear in my face

"There's naught we can do now," he told me. "We must needs live with whatever John Alden can do. Hopefully, he'll be able to get home to Plimoth for our rescue. If there are accusations, it will be on Thomas Prence, our new Plimoth governor, to defend us against the gentry of Boston and their governor, John Winthrop."

Girding my emotions—as if I were pulling my stay-laces tight over my shaky courage—I sought to assure my husband that I had faith in our future. "We can only trust in God, and know it is His will that we are destined to thrive in His promised land." My heart was not as strong as my words, but I turned to clean up the meal, hoping my words would be true.

10

MAY 1634 [SEQUANKEESWUCH/PLANTING CORN]
KOUSSINOC TRADING POST, MAINE

Attitash:

I was left behind when my husband and brother headed south on the trail to Wampanoag territory. My fury at being told by Jon-owland I had to go in the boat was still strong, but I'd had to accept the plan. Esapett's explanation of women's standing in the Strangers' lives, "Our men don't listen to women, like yours do," had proven true over the years.

Jon-owland agreed with Black Whale and Fish Hawk that a woman and three young children traveling on foot would hinder the men's ability to travel swiftly and avoid danger. Although the Abenaki were allies, hostile action was a real threat in a forest that hid murdering Strangers or betraying Narragansett.

"Jon-alden and William Latham are taking the shallop to Boston. They could safely carry you and the children and most of our goods," Black Whale told me. "You can meet us there."

Neither way home was free of risk. "My choice is to endanger you and my brother by traveling with you or to go with Jon-alden—a man I do not trust."

Esapett heard my fears and tried to help. All she could do was persuade her husband to bring Jon-alden and our men to their home to talk. Esapett and I were part of the conversation, but I felt my words were of the same value as my little daughter's. Jon-owland assured me that both Jon-alden and William Latham would protect us.

Esapett told me that despite Jon-alden's lack of attention to my people, he would not abuse me. I listened to her and tried to make my heart agree with her words, but her face revealed she was not certain that he would treat me with respect.

"Stay, Attitash. Parting will come soon enough. I will make tea and we will enjoy this time together." We sat in her room high in Koussinoc. Nippa'uus was going down and we could watch it through the look-out that was made with a shiny cover she called "glass." As the room turned a soft red from the western sky, Esapett built up her fire and put a pot on its hook to seethe. Then she took up two small bottles that were shaped with narrow tops and fat bottoms. They were made of the same glass as the look-out, but almost the color of spring grass. There was sand in one bottle. Esapett tipped the one with sand so that its little top fit on the empty bottle.

"It takes ten minutes for the sand to leave the top bottle and fill the bottom," Esapett said to Nipi and Red Berry. The girls sat on the floor with Esapett's daughters. I had heard Esapett and her daughter talk about minutes and knew it was a short space between this now and the next now. I knew my hands held ten fingers.

"Why ten minutes?" I asked her.

She smiled the quick small smile that made the quiet-water in her eyes sparkle. Then she bit her lip. "It's so I can time—so I know how long to steep the tea, or to let biscuits bake."

For as long as we'd known each other, I still could not understand so many things she said. Red Berry got up and went to watch Esapett closely. "Me do," she said.

Nay, it might break, but good girl to use English," Esapett said. I picked up Red Berry and put her on my hip. It was good we were going home. It would put Red Berry in a confusing spot if she used the Strangers' words.

WHEN BLACK WHALE AND FISH HAWK left, we all openly wept. We could only hope that we would see each other again. Mosk insisted that he could keep up with his father and uncle, and even help carry our bundles. Nipi and Red Berry clung to me. I had to take the children in hand and tell them they were now old enough to accept danger and separation.

The children and I moved back to the Abenaki. Their large village of 500 people had plenty of longhouses with room for us and we would be safe with them until we left with Jonalden. He would not go until their wind canoe could be filled with the furs brought in during the melted-ice time.

The sliver moon took a long time growing to the full Sequankeeswuch—the planting weachimin moon. I did not plant. We would leave before anything could grow.

Saying goodbye to Esapett and her children was not as hard as when Black Whale left, but it would be a long time before we would meet again—if we ever did. I took her hands and looked down into her eyes-like-quiet water. "Fawell, friend— netop," I tried to say. But so much sorrow was in my throat there was no room for words. Esapett looked back up into my eyes. Hers were filled with tears now and I let mine slide down my cheeks. We leaned into each other, brushing cheeks.

"God be with thee, netop—friend." Esapett said.

"All the good spirits keep thee," I said, using her words.

Esapett turned to her husband, who took her in his arms. Her trembling shoulders revealed that his attempts to console her did not stop her weeping.

Pah-scilla did not join in our goodbye. She wept silently when she left her husband's embrace. Esapett shook off her own tears and put an arm around Pah-scilla, gently leading her back to her children.

I set my own shoulders straight and turned my attention to getting Mosk, Nipi and Red Berry safely on the little wind canoe. We stowed our bundles, then stood with our faces downstream, away from our friends.

D*URING THE VOYAGE* to Boston, Jon-alden and I managed to stay out of each other's way. If I needed anything that I couldn't find myself, William Latham helped me. The wind gods were good to us and most days they gave us enough of their breath without blowing big waves. At night, the men took down the white cloth sail and fastened it taut across part of the boat so we could sleep beneath. There was plenty of space between us, filled with my belongings, but I could hear Jon-alden and William Latham breathing whenever I woke up. Only by softly singing a prayer could I go back to sleep.

When Nippa'uus rose the third morning, I got up from under the sail, took my son with me and left everyone else sleeping. As I stood praying to welcome the light, Jon-alden came to pull the sail into position. He ignored us, as usual, until I finished singing my prayer. When I looked at Jon-alden again, he had turned to watch my son and his face was no longer a stone. Mosk had gotten up and was standing on a chest so he could pee over the edge of the boat. Jon-alden smiled at my son. "Nancompees," he said. Alden had used our word for 'boy.' Mosk finished relieving himself and smiled back at Alden. From that point on, I did not try to avoid Jon-alden.

Elisabeth:

Priscilla Alden was a strong woman. I'd always looked up to her and leaned on her. But now she crumpled in my arms, as the shallop carrying her husband, William Latham, Attitash and her children, and the others, was out of sight down-stream. My John went with us as we walked back to the fort and stayed until her tears were dried. We promised Priscilla we'd be there for anything she wanted, then left her with her five children.

That night, even before our children quieted down in their bedding on the floor, I snuggled close to John and whispered, "Do ye believe we'll get through this?"

"We have tonight. Let's not worry about other nights," he replied softly.

We'd left the shutters open, needing the late May breezes more than we feared night creatures. The hoot of an owl was in my dream and I thought it was telling me where to find John. I woke up, but it was still hooting. The full moon filled our room in the top floor with light. My husband's sleeping face was turned toward me. Softly, so as not to wake him, I brushed my lips across his cheek. He responded slowly with his hands, then kissed me tenderly. Passion seized both of us and by the time his tongue touched mine, I was already slippery. Biting my tongue to keep from crying out, I urged his immediate entry. He turned onto his back and brought me to lean over him. I took off my night cap to let my hair brush his face.

"Thy face looks just like thee did when we first lay together," he whispered.

My small laugh bubbled out, impossible to hold in as he moved beneath me. "That's because ye see me by moonlight."

"Nay, it's because I see thee inside, in thy soul."

I could not hold back my passion and when John's surged, I joined him. My tears released unbidden. My body shook with both joy and despair. This night would end. I could not avoid the future. John held me and I wept silently until sleep again claimed me.

When I woke in the morning, alone in my bed, I thought at first that the midnight love-making was a sweet dream.

Knowing how much pleasure I'd felt, I realized I might get with child again. What if I had six children to raise after their father was jailed or hanged? My tight shoulders blades pulled away from my body so I could hardly take a breath. I sat up and forced air into my fear. Whatever befell, I would have to carry on. Whatever God gave me, I would accept. Pulling aside my bed curtains, I greeted my children. John had already brought water from the spring. Time to start another day. A day with all my family present and hungry.

11

Attitash:

Boston was the busiest village I had ever seen. Many big wind canoes crowded the shore. There was much confusion as Jon-alden and William Latham pulled down the white cloth and used the long paddles to reach the shore.

There were many houses and people, but I could not see even one Wampanoag face. How could we be in Wampanoag territory? When we had journeyed north to Abenaki territory, we'd not gone near this new Strangers' village. We knew the Strangers had taken over a Wampanoag village in which most of our people had already died of the Strangers' diseases. Jon-alden told me there were 300 people living in Plimoth and 4,000 in Boston. I had no idea what that number meant, but I could tell it was far more than anyone could count.

"Who counts them?" I'd asked.

Jon-alden shrugged. "Maybe they just count the houses and make a guess about how many in each house."

Now, a Stranger on shore called to Jon-alden. His big nose was as red as the sour berries. William Latham told me that Red Nose would haul our goods across the Big Salt Water. I'd hoped Black Whale and Fish Hawk would have arrived already, but they were not waiting at the place Jon-alden called 'the wharf.'

When we left Koussinoc to go back down the Kennebec, I'd hated being on this wind canoe. But now I did not want to leave it. At least, in the wind canoe, I could avoid all the new Strangers. My chest felt as though it had been circled by ropes—as the kidnappers had done so many years ago. I stood on the dock, breathing hard and getting my land legs back while also reassuring the children, who hid behind me.

Jon-alden and William Latham began unloading the goods. William called out, "I see Black Whale."

Good air rushed into my body and I laughed with relief as my husband's head showed above the shorter Strangers crowded on the street. Before he could reach me, two Strangers dressed in colorful cloth pushed ahead of him. The Strangers shoved me and my children aside and moved toward Jon-alden. He looked up from his work and it appeared he greeted the Strangers. A useless greeting, as the Strangers took Jon-alden by the wrists and tied them with a rope. I could not understand what the Strangers said to Jon-alden, but their voices sounded like bears growling.

"On what charge?" Jon-alden asked in a voice pitched high with anger.

I tried to translate but could not find the meaning. Their answer did not make sense either, although I'd heard the word.

"Murder."

I ran over to where Mosk was sitting. "We must get out *now!*" I said, trying to keep my words steady. I snatched the little girls in their cradleboards and looked around for Black Whale. He came to me and told Mosk to help with my bundles.

"What about Jon-alden?" he asked.

"We can't help," I said.

Black Whale looked back at William Latham on the wind canoe. As we ran, he told me that Fish Hawk would be waiting beyond the houses. We pushed through the crowd. I did not understand all the words, but "savages" and "Satan's own" were spewing out so often that I knew they were hateful. Mean faces told their own story.

The little girls were whimpering. Mosk ran behind me, where he could keep the little ones in sight. I could not hear much above the crowd, but when a lull came, Mosk's words to the girls, "Don't cry," came through.

After we found Fish Hawk, we kept going until we could no longer see Boston. He had located a place with a spring and made camp. By weaving leafy branches over two young saplings bent into an arc, we made a cover for sleeping. Fish Hawk had caught some fish and even snared some rabbits to cook. Black Whale told Fish Hawk what happened to Jon-alden while I cooked.

It was almost impossible to keep bad spirits from residing in my head. The Strangers were endangering our very lives. But I was so weary when we bedded down before dark that I went to sleep without trying to know what to do next.

It was still dark when I was startled half awake and looked around. Were we in danger? I could not hear or see anything. Dreams with confusing images still swirled in my head—Seafoam calling me and my trying to answer. That dream was followed by one in which Jon-alden and William Latham were in a boat headed for a waterfall. Esapett and I called to them, but they could not hear over the noise of the water.

As the dream faded, I listened to my children breathe. Would they survive this new trouble? There must be a way to keep these Boston strangers from harming my family and Esapett's. Looking at my sleeping children, I remembered a time before these Strangers invaded. They were all invaders. Not only these Boston people, not only Allerton and Billington. My heart shriveled and my belly felt like it was being wrung out. Oh, the life our grandmothers told about their grandmothers—our land, the Big Salt Water, the trees, the springs, the wampum. We and all Kiehtan's creatures lived here together: bear, wolves, beaver, otter, fish, and whales. The life we lost. "I despise them." I wept quietly. "My heart cannot hold any of them." I bit my tongue—I had almost said "Not even Esapett."

I dared not go back to sleep—worse dreams might possess me. I waited until Nippa'uus rose, then hurried through a quick meal. We needed to get far away from Boston.

We walked until Nippa'uus was high, then stopped by a spring to get water and eat some journey cake.

"When we get to Plimoth," Black Whale said, "our friends will have to figure out how to get Jon-alden out of the cage and the shallop back to Maine with the trading goods." He looked worried. "By putting Jon-alden behind bars, it means these same people are plotting against our friends." Black Whale gripped my hand. "We must help before these enemies attack Jon-owland or try to lure him to Boston."

"How can we warn Jon-owland and Esapett?" I asked.

"Maybe a Massachuseuk could carry a message to the Abenaki and get it to the trading post." My husband's eyes were tight, almost hidden beneath his drawn brows. "That is, if we can find one who's friendly."

"Where would we find a Massachuseuk?" I asked. "We have to go to Plimoth."

"Ahhe, and we'd better start walking. But we'll stay on this trail the Massachuseuk use."

The trail grew narrow and we let the little girls down to stretch their legs. Having lived little more than two circle of seasons, they could not walk far. Red Berry's innocent smiling face as she babbled with Nipi, caught my thoughts.

When she grew older, I would tell her about Moses Ta-bot, the good, kind, Stranger who was her mother's husband. Red Berry would not need to know that the man who planted his seed in Seafoam was Hocking, one of the invaders. Nor would I tell her about Shimmering Fish, her mother's first husband who was Wampanoag. And Red Berry would learn enough about the Narragansett without needing to know they had also abused her mother.

Elisabeth:

"What could make them so late?" I asked John when eight days had come and gone without word from the travelers. Instead of answering, he closed his eyes.

We could not pretend there was no cause for concern. If there had not been trouble, Alden and Latham would have unloaded all the furs, packed up all the cloth, blankets, rugs, knives, beads, and gun powder from England and immediately set sail back to the Kennebec river. They would have been back to us by now. If news of the Talbot and Hocking deaths had reached Boston, it could lead to accusations of murder. I dared not suggest that John Alden and William Latham might be held hostage in order for the enemy poachers to demand my husband's presence in Boston.

"Last night I dreamed about Alden and Latham," he said, breaking the silence. "They were both in a Boston Court, being spat on by the Governor and Boston gentry." When he opened his eyes, they showed a glistening of tears. "I go over and over the events. I know it does no good, and I know God is watching over all of us." He lifted his shoulders and rolled them back, letting out the kinks. "But I can't let go of my regret, wondering what could have been different. My men and I were accosted by the scoundrels and took action. Now we are in a desperate situation."

"Ye must not feel that way." I needed to assure my beloved but hesitated to express my thoughts. John listened when I offered counsel, but rarely asked me for it. We were in a new place in our marriage, brought closer together by events, so that I no longer kept such a close lid on my thoughts or my passion. "We both understand that only God knows what

He ordains. Our own ideas are an attempt to understand this brief mortal life." I paused, saddened by the memories. "So many have died."

Our children came in from the garden, and we dropped the conversation.

Attitash:

We were not sure we could get to Plimoth before evening but we kept walking. The sound of movement on the trail ahead stopped us. Black Whale handed Mosk to me and walked around the bend. He came back, followed by three Massachuseuk men. They greeted us without visible animosity. When they learned why we had been in Boston, their mouths turned down.

"Boston is a bad place with bad people. Many more than in Plimoth. They would never make a treaty like the Clothmen in Plimoth made with you." The Massachuscuk man spat onto the ground. "One of the Boston sachems—called Jon-Win-tip—told his people their great spirit killed all of our people with their 'pox' so they could have our land." The Massachuseuk said that only a small number of their people were still alive. "Their sachem proclaims this is the will of the spirit they call 'The Cur-ist.' Stay away from Boston."

I wondered if these Massachuseuk were telling the truth or a tale to keep us out of their territory. Black Whale rubbed his topknot, repositioning the feather. I knew he was determining whether to believe them. He glanced at me and I nodded my head. These men were our only hope to get word up north to Esapett and Jon-owland.

"Will you take a message to the Abenaki?" Black Whale asked. "They could find the Clothman, Jon-owland, who's at the Kennebec River trading post—Koussinoc."

When they hesitated, he counted out a few wampum beads. Black Whale took out one of his knives with his own mark carved into the handle. He explained the Massachuseuk had to give his knife to Jon-owland. Speaking very slowly, with the Massachuseuk repeating twice after him, Black Whale said, 'Jon-owland,' then 'Jon-alden.' He had them repeat, "In prison in Boston. Plimoth Clothmen come to help." He picked up some sticks and held them in front of his face, showing how the Strangers held Jon-alden in a cage, so the Massachuseuk could demonstrate to Jon-owland.

After repeating two more times, the Massachuseuk put the knife and wampum in their journey bags and went their way. We chanted prayers for their safe journey and for the message to be understood.

We continued walking but stopped again when we heard the clop-clop of a horse coming from Plimoth. We laughed with relief when the light brown nose of Papa's horse appeared with Fish Hawk's head leaning over its neck.

"Plimoth has a new sachem—Puh-rence." He slid off the horse and gave the leather strap to Mosk. "He and the other leaders talk of sending Cap-an San-dish to Boston with men and arms."

Fish Hawk put Mosk behind him on Papa's horse. Black Whale and I carried both girls and the packs. We moved quickly now, watching Nippa'uus sinking behind the western hills. After four circles of seasons, my heart went ahead of me to my family. It was still light out when we arrived at my family's homesite.

When I held my sister and mother again, tears overflowed so that I could hardly see. Their arms and their scent filled my heart. Then Mama finally turned to greet her grandchildren.

My children hung back at first. Nipi had been born in Koussinoc, so had never seen her grandparents and aunt. Mosk, though he hardly remembered them, accepted their embrace. Relief welled up, soothing my worries.

Mama and Papa looked at Red Berry with raised eyebrows. I introduced her to them as "Aunt and Uncle," and said quietly that Seafoam was her mother. "She disappeared. She's gone to the Spirit World, we believe."

Red Berry was too little to understand, but let Mama pick her up.

"She needs to meet her grandparents," Mama said, putting the child down again. "We will send word to Seafoam's parents. First Star and my brother, Red Hawk, will come take the child home to the Beaver Clan fire."

When I finally told my children it was time to sleep, Nipi looked up at the stars and Towwankeeswuch—the 'hill the corn' moon—and said "Look, Mama. The moon followed us all the way here!"

I kissed her. "Yes, my Nipi, the moon watches over you wherever you are."

"Does the moon follow me too?" Red Berry asked. "Even when I go to my grandmother's home?"

"Moon follows all of us. You too," I assured Red Berry. She went to sleep with a smile on her little face.

We sat by a small fire outside. The fireflies blinked in the near woods. I told Mama Seafoam's story, including that the man Ta-bot—whom Fish Hawk had told them was murdered—was Seafoam's husband. I did not mention that he was not the Clothman who fathered Red Berry. Hocking's seed was not worthy of being revealed.

"But of course, she is Beaver Clan, like her mother." Mama responded. We knew that was all that mattered. "Seafoam's brother, Silver Fish, will be a good Clan Uncle to Red Berry."

Papa told us about the new Plimoth sachem, Tomas Puh-rence. "Our good friend, Edward Win-sow went across the Big Salt Water to their old home. Tomas Puh-rence became sachem in Plimoth, three moons ago. You may have heard that about the same time, Strangers in Boston chose a new sachem, Thomas Dud-ey, to replace Sachem Jon-wintop."

I could not keep up with the confusion of Clothmen's names.

Papa continued, "Before he left, Edward Win-sow told me what this Sachem Jon-wintop had said. I repeated it many times, so I would not forget what an evil man led the people of Boston." Papa paused, "Maybe the new Boston sachem is not as evil, but I doubt that."

Black Whale and I waited until Papa put down the pipe he'd taken from Mama. "Edward Win-sow told me just a few of the words Jon-wintop used. He said so many words people could not understand him." Papa closed his eyes, bringing the strange words back. "He said 'By what right have we to take that land which has belonged to these people?'" Papa opened his eyes, "So I thought this Cloth-man understood this is our land. But then Edward Win-sow told me the rest of it: 'God killed the natives with a plague so the Cloth-men could have the land.'"

The back of my neck turned ice cold. Long ago, Tisquantum had told us the Strangers' god sent a plague to kill us. And most of our people did die of evil spirits' disease. But so many of the Strangers died, too, that we believed Bad-ford, Win-sow, and even Jon-owland, when they told us that their gods sent the bad spirit plagues and pox to all people, not just us. Did Esapett not know the truth? Or did she hide the truth from me? No friend would do that.

My family waited as Black Whale and I absorbed the fear-some news of the Boston Strangers who made the decisions. I tried to breathe, but the air came tangled up in my lungs, like my hair when I washed it and did not braid it up imme-diately. My husband took my hand and I gripped his. I took long, slow breaths until my body calmed the air.

"Will any of our Plimoth Strangers go to rescue Jon-al-den?" I asked Mama.

"Ahhe, they will go in their wind-canoe in the morning."

12

Elisabeth:

The first two weeks my bedtime prayers were the same fervent wish every night—that John Alden and William Latham would return, full of good news. After that, my prayer included Attitash and Black Whale. Without word from John Alden, we had no way of knowing if they and their children had reached home safely.

One night I dreamed that little Nipi, Red Berry, and Mosk were playing 'ring around the rosy' with our children. The song was from the plague and the children-killing small poxe. Ashes were all that was left after their bodies were burned to destroy the disease.

Struggling awake, I thought of the letters that had come on the last boat from Plimoth. Edward Winslow had written that both the Brewsters' daughters—Fear and Patience—had died of the small poxe.

"This letter shows God gives the poxe and the plague to all of us—not just the heathen," Edward Winslow had written, after informing us of the deaths. "The governor at Massachusetts Bay Colony chooses to believe otherwise." As evidence, Edward Winslow had written out quotes from Governor John

Winthrop. To understand the meaning, I'd had to read the passages twice.

It was early morning and John was still asleep. My memory of Governor Winthrop's words nagged me, so I got up and fumbled in the trunk to find the letters. The first quote was in a letter that Massachusetts governor, John Winthrop had written in 1630, the year Boston was founded.

> *This savage people ruleth over many lands without title or property; for they inclose no ground, neither have they cattell to maintayne it .....And why may no Christians have liberty to go and dwell amongst them in their waste lands and woods...as lawfully as Abraham did among the Sodomites?...., God hath consumed the natives with a miraculous plague, wherby the greater part of the country is left voide of inhabitants.*

The next quote, written just a few months ago, in 1634.

> *"But for the natives in these parts, God's hand hath so pursued them as for 300 miles space, the greatest parte of them are swept away by the small poxe, which still continues among them: So God hathe hereby cleared our title to this place.*

Governor John Winthrop's words were all too familiar. I'd heard Isaac Allerton and others say more or less the same thing—that God destroyed the Indians with the diseases so we could have this bountiful land. I could not help wondering if the heathens who are our friends—even Attitash—despised and feared us for bringing this pestilence.

Winthrop, Allerton and their kind are such cruel fools! I was so distressed that I spoke out loud, without thinking of my sleeping family. They ignore all our deaths and take pleasure in the loss of the people, "native in these parts," as

Winthrop calls them. The Boston governor is beyond cruel!
He might take Attitash and Black Whale prisoner—or kill
them! I now whispered, as if to say it out loud would make it
true. What will he do with John Alden and William Latham?
Even if the governor is restrained, our friends are in the hands
of greedy, evil men in the Massachusetts Bay Colony!

Attitash:

San-dish's men made so much noise we were disturbed from
our late sleep.

"Did you hear the noisy skins they call drums?" Papa almost smiled. "It was a good laugh to watch them strut. They
marched out with their firesticks in their arms, all in rows—
like the way they plant the weachimin."

"Can we catch up with them before they get to Boston?"
Black Whale asked my father and Fish Hawk.

"Why would you go to such a dangerous place?" Papa
asked.

"San-dish's men just know how to point their firesticks
and shoot," Black Whale answered. "If they shoot, the Boston
Strangers might kill Jon-alden."

"Do you care if Jon-alden is killed? Is it worth risking your
own lives?" Mama asked.

"You test my understanding, wife's mother," Black Whale
replied. We were accustomed to Mama making sure the men
knew what they were doing. I waited for Black Whale's answer. "These Boston Strangers are our biggest danger," Black
Whale's voice rose. "If they succeed in keeping Jon-alden in
the cage, or worse, our people could lose our lands."

"But the danger to you!" Mama said.

I knew that my husband and brother, like all warriors
would put themselves in danger to save the rest of us.

"The Boston Strangers won't recognize us if we dress like
them," Black Whale assured her.

Papa declared he would go with Black Whale and Fish Hawk. Mama, White Flower, and I sang the courage prayer for them as we refreshed their bags with journey cake. They removed all their paint and feathers, putting on Clothmen shirts that Papa always wore when he accompanied the Plimoth men taking goods to Boston. High upon horses above the crowd and wearing Clothman hats, shirts, leggings and each carrying a firestick, our men could blend in.

Elisabeth:

There was nothing to be gained by dwelling on the grim possibilities of Attitash and her family. We continued to plod through the day, our eyes straying to the river hoping for the sight of the shallop's sail.

One day a small party of Abenaki men appeared who were not from the village. Priscilla and I were hanging washing out on the bushes to dry. John put down his wood-splitting mallet and greeted them. I brought the water bucket and the Abenaki men cupped their hands to receive the drink. When I had poured for each of the three, the tallest one drew a package from his journey bag. He unwrapped the deerskin and revealed a small knife. It had a wooden handle and a quahog-shell blade.

John examined the markings on the handle. "Black Whale's knife!"

"Ahhe, Black Whale." The man nodded in affirmation. "Black Whale give to Massachuseuck. He give to them and they bring to us—Abenaki. To tell Jon-owland."

John kept his eyes on the Abenaki. "Tell me what?"

"Black Whale in Boston. Black Whale captive."

John became alarmed, "Is Black Whale all right?"

The Abenaki shrugged their shoulders. "All we know is message we give."

"Did they say anything about John Alden?" he asked.

"All we know is message we give," he repeated.

John drew out his old pen knife that he used to trim the quill. He spit on his mark on its handle, then rubbed it. He handed the knife to the Abenaki man.

"Find a Massachuseuk, tell him to look for Wampanoag and go to Plimoth. Give my knife to Bradford or Winslow and tell them Black Whale is captured."

The Abenaki men murmured to each other. They no doubt knew that more than ten years ago there had been bad blood between our leaders in Plimoth and the Massachuseuk. Weston's men had so abused the Massachuseuk that it harmed our own relationship with the Massachuseuk.

The tall Abenaki finally accepted John's knife, repeated his instructions, first saying, "Go to Boston" instead of Plimoth. By the third repetition, he got it right and the group left quickly, following a path that led below the Kennebec waterfall to connect with the trail.

"Will they be able to keep the message straight all the way back home to Plimoth?" I asked John.

"It's all in God's hands." John replied. He watched the trail as if his eyes could see the hidden path the Abenaki took. "This is very curious," he said as he turned back to me. "Why did they know nothing about John Alden? Why did they put Black Whale in jail? Did Black Whale get another gun?" He did not wait for an answer. Neither of us had any way of knowing. "If he got a gun from Hopkins, or someone else in Plimoth, the Boston officials may have found it."

"It wouldn't take a gun to make their evil governor do harm to him," I said. I could only imagine what small pretense the governor would contrive to imprison Black Whale.

John's eyes were as dark as the green forest near sunset—as they always were when his thoughts filled his head. We stood outside, watching an eagle soar in ever higher circles above the river. "If only we could fly and look down on Boston!" he finally said.

I was not sure I wanted to see what was happening in Boston.

Attitash

With Black Whale, Fish Hawk and Papa gone to Boston, our homesite seemed empty. I wondered if the Massachuseuk had delivered our message about Jon-alden, Jon-owland and Esa-pett.

Mama and I went down to the shore that night. It was good to be on the familiar shore of the Big Salt Water again after four circles of seasons. The A-rocks still separated our homesite shore from Plimoth. We went past the boundary rock to see if we might get word of what was going on in Boston.

Mary Chi-ton Win-sow and Con-sance Hopkins Snow were there with their children. The children had grown, just as my Mosk had. None seemed surprised to see me. No doubt Fish Hawk had brought news of our return. My brother had grown from a boy to a man since we left, but they must have recognized him.

Both women spoke politely to me, looking with smiles at my Nipi, but their questions were all about Esapett and Pah-scilla. I could only tell them that when we left Koussi-noc—a long moon ago—both were well but anxious about Jon-Alden.

"I hope Captain Standish can prove to those Boston big-wigs they must free Alden," Con-sance said. She bit her lip and I saw tears glimmer in her eyes. "Mary's husband and mine are with Standish."

"My husband and brother went to Boston again, with my father," I said.

Mary responded with eyes widened in surprise. "But is that not dangerous for your people? Boston does not accept you like most in Plimoth do." She looked at me with kind eyes. Boston was dangerous, but it seemed everywhere that the Strangers lived was dangerous. I should not have told Mary my father and husband were in Boston—she might tell others in Plimoth. Hopefully, no one knew our men were dressed like Clothmen and carried firesticks.

Mary gathered her children and, with a quick farewell to Con-sance, left the shore.

"Mary and John Winslow, her husband, are talking about moving to Boston," Con-sance told me. "There is better trade there, lots more of us Christians, and hardly any Massachuseuk left." Her eyes were friendly, but her words troubling. "She knows what it is like there. Here in Plimoth the tide is also turning," she added, as she too gathered her children and left.

I looked out to the Big Salt Water, knowing the word 'tide' meant when the sea came in to shore, then left again. It was at its usual place just before Nippa'uus went down. I understood little else that Con-sance said. Hopefully, she meant our men would be back soon.

Elisabeth:

John pulled me against him, holding me close so my body molded into his. "God has either cooked up a very strange pot for us, or Satan has completely taken over."

"Then we must pray for strength." I turned my head so it fit against his shoulder.

"And for patience," he said.

Easier said than done, I thought to myself. "God's will can only be revealed in good time."

"We must not mention this to Priscilla yet," John added. "She need not fret more than she already is." It startled me that my husband was worrying about Priscilla.

Our four oldest children slept soundly on the floor. Only Lydia, the baby, slept between us and did not seem to notice her father shifting from one side to the other. I reached across the baby to put my hand on John's shoulder. His warmth soothed me to sleep.

I was traveling with John, though where or how did not seem relevant. All I knew was I was in a town larger than Boston, mayhap London, and I now could not find my husband. Someone called to me from a large house. "Your husband is here." With great relief I entered the house and was shown into a large room. John was lying on his back on the carpeted floor, his chained hands folded over his body.

"You can stay here with him," said the man who'd brought me in.

John's eyes were closed and I could not tell if he was sick, hurt, or dying. I noted his chest rising and falling. As I knelt by my husband and laid hands on his shoulders, I wondered who would care for my children while I kept watch. It did not seem strange in my dream that Priscilla now appeared at my side. Nor did it seem strange that she told me she would sit with my husband while I went to care for my children. But something made me turn to look one last time at my darling as I got up to leave and saw my friend, Priscilla, leaning over to kiss my husband.

Forcing shallow breaths in an attempt to wake up, I reached across for John, but he was not there. My stomach fluttered as the dream clung to me. Little Lydia stirred and I snuggled her next to me. Hearing movement, I sat up to see John coming in the door.

"Where were ye?"

"Just getting water." He looked at my face in the dim light. "Are ye all right?"

Guilt nudged me that I should dream about my friend and my husband.

"Now I am."

I realized I should check on Priscilla as soon as I got the porridge ready.

PRISCILLA'S FACE WAS PALE, with dark circles under her eyes showing both her worry and her age. Her oldest boy could get the water, but that did not ease her worry that her husband was in danger.

"Trust in God, Priscilla," I murmured, embracing her. "He will surely bring thy husband back."

"I do trust in God, Elisabeth," she answered. "But we can't know what His will is and I might not like it." She turned to her babe, fussed with its skirts, and then lifted it up. "I must prepare myself for the worst—that my own John will not return."

"Do ye believe the worst?" I asked, imploring her not to.

Priscilla put the struggling child back down to toddle about. "I don't know what I believe." Tears slipped from her eyes and she wiped them with her cuff, at first ignoring my offered hand, then grabbing onto it so tight that my fingers buzzed. "If I don't prepare myself for the worst and I become a widow, I won't have the strength to carry on my duty as a mother."

As I walked to our rooms, my fitful mind turned to the many stories in the Bible of men marrying their wives' sisters. It was common then to take care of widows by taking multiple wives. I shook off the thought just as I had earlier shaken off the dream.

Attitash:

I woke before Nippa'uus. I was there to welcome the light, praying that our men would return. I had just finished first meal, when Fish Hawk arrived.

"They come behind me," he said as he slid off the horse. Relief spilled out of my body with a small cry.

"And what of Jon-alden?"

"Ahhe, I will tell you." Fish Hawk sat down by our fire, knowing a good story does not waste the ending by putting the last first. "By the time we came to Latham on the small wind-canoe, we'd already seen Captain Standish and the men with him. We found them just outside Boston, setting up camp. We revealed ourselves to Standish, who told us they went right up to the place where John Alden was held. Drum beating-tat, tat, tat...tatta tat."

This sounded like a tale with a good ending. My son, Mosk, was listening. Fish Hawk noticed and pulled his clan nephew close.

Fish Hawk took a long drink. "Black Whale and I stepped into the shadows when the big Boston sachem came out—no doubt the drum and the sight of all our Plimoth men with their firesticks pointed to the sky made an entrance he could not ignore."

Fish Hawk took another bowl of food. We waited for more.

Mama finally asked, "What happened next?"

"The Boston sachem told Captain he had to talk to someone else who'd seen the incident. If the story matched, John Alden would be released in the morning." Fish Hawk stopped to eat more. "We told Standish we knew where William Latham was and we'd bring him to tell the story. Standish strutted like a turkey, shouting at Sachem Dudley, 'We have a witness and will bring him forthwith.'"

"We left and went to the small wind canoe, they call 'shallop'. No one paid attention and we came safely on board." He took another big helping of venison stew and we waited while he ate.

"After we told William he would have to go speak, we helped him finish loading the rest of our furs onto the tall boat next to us on the dock." Fish Hawk continued. "The white-cloth Strangers just watched us. The one with a big red nose seemed to be in charge."

I'd seen a White-Cloth Stranger with a red nose when Jon-alden brought me to Boston. He had talked with Jon-alden about carrying our trading goods across the Big Salt Water.

Fish Hawk wiped his mouth and settled back.

"The tall boat was waiting to sail until more trade goods arrived. William Latham left us guarding his shallop and went to find the Boston sachem at the jail where they kept Alden. It was a long day. It was almost dark when William finally came back. After asking the guards at the jail, William found Sachem Dudley in a big house near the jail. Standish had left most of his men camped but brought a few back to be with William when he told his story. William told Sachem Dudley that he'd been in Koussinoc with Howland."

My brother stopped to take a few long breaths. He looked up at Nippa'uus, high in the sky, then continued.

"At first, the Sachem did not want to listen to William. Standish began shouting again, with his men pointing their firesticks. The Sachem Dudley finally let William talk. William told how Hocking shot Talbot in the face and then shots came from Talbot's friends and Hocking was killed. Sachem Dudley talked to his men, then finally announced he would release John Alden the next morning if he promised he would sail straight back to Koussinoc." Fish Hawk stretched his arms above his head and rolled his shoulders.

"When will Black Whale and Papa come home?" I asked. It was a relief that Jon-alden was to be set free, but Fish Hawk had not told me what my heart needed to hear—why my husband and our father had not come home with him.

"Black Whale and Papa went to where John Alden was caged. They said they would watch his release from the cage and see him safely back to his small wind canoe. I rode ahead so I could bring word to you. They planned to shed their Clothmen clothes after they left Boston and ride fast. They should be here soon."

Fish Hawk sounded so sure, but he was still just sixteen.

He was too young to think of what might happen to us. In the time it took to tell his story, the Boston Clothmen could discover Black Whale and Papa. There would not be an end to my brother's story until all of us were safely back at home.

13

Attitash:

All day I listened for the footsteps of horses. Nippa'uus went behind the hills. Dark came. But my husband and father had not appeared. Fish Hawk still did not seem worried.

"They were probably waiting until Jon-Alden and William set sail for Koussinoc," he said. That was not good enough for me. Every heartbeat felt like someone was pounding journey cake on my chest.

All night, I listened. I could no longer wait like a child. I had to go find Black Whale and Papa. Before Nippa'uus rose, I got up. It was easy to explain to my mother. She usually hid her fears better than I, but she was also worried. Mama helped me find another set of Clothmen's clothes in the storage bags. She assured me she would keep my children busy so they would not worry.

Mama gave me her horse, a small, surefooted mare. Insisting it would raise an alarm if I rode the horse bareback, she went to the big house where the Strangers' kept their horses and took a hard riding-seat they call 'saddle.'

"I will tell Brewster later that I borrowed it," she smiled.

Nippa'uus was low in the eastern sky above the Big Salt Water when I left for Boston. It hurt my bottom to sit on the saddle for so long. I worried that my feet would tangle in the slings they call 'stirrups,' so I slid my feet out and used my thighs to stay on the horse.

It was a long ride, longer than I thought it would take. My hope was that I would meet Black Whale and Papa on the trail. All I encountered were deer, a curious porcupine, and squirrels. As I approached Boston, I grew more afraid. Had Black Whale and Papa been put in a cage when the soldiers let Jon-alden out? I tried to tell myself that my husband and father were on the small wind-canoe with William Latham, waiting for Jon-alden's return. Or maybe he had and they were all telling their stories.

When I came into the village, I kept my beaver Clothmen's hat down and kept my horse at a brisk trot. I worked my way past houses on hard rock roads until I could see the water reflecting Nippa'uus. I hoped Black Whale and Papa would be with the small wind canoe.

My horse slowed as we arrived at the dock—there was no small wind-canoe, only a tall one. A Clothman was standing on the dock, leaning against the board they use to get up to the tall wind-canoe. My heart squeezed tight and I leaned onto my horse's neck, trying to gain strength from her warmth. The mare twitched her head, which knocked my hat back, exposing my face and freeing my braids. As I reached over my shoulder to stick my braids back under my hat, the borrowed shirt snugged tight against my breasts.

"Yur not a man!" He used their words, but I understood.

As I shoved my hat tight, the Clothman pushed his own cap back and I saw his red nose.

His eyes opened wide. "Yur the maid who came on the shallop with men from the Kennebec."

I nodded and pulled the brim of my hat lower.

"Whacha doin' here?" His eyes were slants and his mouth

a tight line. "Git out before the soldiers come."

He did not seem one to ask questions of, so I said nothing.

"If yur looking for Christians—the one called Alden and his man sailed to Maine this morning." He pointed out to the Big Salt Water as if I were able to see what the birds and fish saw out there. I nodded but did not move. He sensed what I really wanted to know.

"Lookin' fer savage men?" Red Nose asked.

I nodded again. Although my head and my heart were spinning, my horse obeyed my hands on her reins and stood still.

The red-nosed Stranger hesitated.

"Where are they?" I asked.

"Tie yur horse," he said, and pointed to the ring where they tied small canoes.

"Where are they?" I demanded again, as I wrapped my horse's reins through the ring.

"Come."

I followed him, my hat so far down over my face I could hardly see his feet.

Red Nose climbed up a ladder onto his tall wind-canoe and I followed. When we got to the deck, a wail escaped my throat. Black Whale and Papa were lying close to each other, against the side of the ship. Their bodies were limp, eyes closed. Papa's face was bloated and covered with bruises. His skin was gray.

I stumbled to them and lifted Black Whale's head into my arms. Feeling a bump on the back of his head, I touched it gingerly and he groaned. I could see movement in his chest, but had to put my head to his mouth to hear his breath. "Black Whale!—Black Whale—Black Whale....."

He struggled to breathe and his eyes fluttered. I looked to Papa. No sign of breath in his chest or throat. The bruises disfigured his face. Placing my hand on my father's mouth, I felt nothing. My heart felt like I'd been left in a snow cave in winter. Cold everywhere. Leaning into my father's face, I breathed on his mouth. It was like breathing into a hole. Holding my sobs, I returned to my husband. He was breathing. But for how long?

"Who did this?" I demanded of Red Nose.

He shifted from side to side. "Boston soldiers come. Saw yur men were Injun. Pissed they were wearing our clothes. Found their guns." Red Nose spit out a vile wad. "The Boston soldiers stole yur men's horses. Threw yur men over the side."

"Noooooo." I shook with despair. Rolling my shoulders to ease my anger's grip, I turned my attention to my Black Whale again. His breath came in rasps.

"After we fished yur men out of the drink," Red Nose looked down on my father and husband with a slight smile, as if he'd landed a catch of fish. "Got the young 'un to cough up water. Older injun might not be breathing."

"That older man is my father!" I put my hands on Papa's chest and pulsed them like my own heart was beating. His chest rose slightly with a shallow breath when I stopped.

Red Nose shrugged one shoulder. "I kin only keep 'em if they be quiet and don't need nothin." He didn't see the horror I was trying to contain in my belly. "Ya gotta git 'em out'a here. If yur pa don't live, we'll bury 'im at sea."

Outrage flooded my veins. The Strangers would pay for this! Red Nose, the Boston soldiers, all the Clothmen in Boston, Jon-alden—wherever he was—all the Strangers in Plimoth, and all the Strangers in Koussinoc. Esapett. Jon-owland.

I leaned into Black Whale's face and spoke into his ear. "Don't leave me."

Elisabeth:

As I walked home, contemplating Priscilla's need to plan for the worst case possible, the wind intensified. Rain was sure to follow. A tree flung its branches in my path. Another branch crashed down right behind me. I could hardly open my door before the wind pushed it back shut. I got it open slightly and our daughter Hope tried to help from the inside. I leaned against the doorframe and pulled hard, nearly falling over when it opened wide. I ducked into my house as the door slammed shut behind me.

"Mother, have you seen Father and Brother John?" Hope's bright green eyes flashed too much worry for a five-year-old.

I looked at the children. They waited for my answer with anxious faces.

"Are they not home yet?" I asked. They shook their heads and then cringed as a crash sent dirt floating down from the sod roof, falling between cracks in the logs.

Baby Lydia began to wail.

Attitash:

"Nipi!!" I commanded Red Nose.

He stood rooted to the boards as if he did not understand me. I realized that I had used our Wampanoag word for water.

"Water. Water!" I motioned drinking water. I needed to mix herbs with water for a remedy to force coughing. Only that would clear out the sea water

He did not respond. I saw a bucket tied to a pole with a water dipper and picked up the dipper. "Water." Red Nose motioned to another man to pour water for me into a small pot.

After I shed my Clothman shirt, leaving the pants under my deerskin dress, I took out my journey bag. Sifting through the dried herbs, I found boneset. It works to clear breathing, but it had to be seethed. Under the dried plants was the fresh watercress I had just picked yesterday when I was at the spring. That only needed to be mixed with cold water and I could dose Black Whale and Papa immediately

"Send someone to find Cap-an San-dish," I told Red

Nose. He looked me straight in the eyes—was his rudeness due to his lack of understanding what I demanded or simply his refusal to do what a savage woman tells him? "I did not meet the Cap-an and his men on the path, so they must still be in Boston." The blank look on the Strangers' faces made me search for more of their words. "Plimoth warriors." I motioned carrying a firestick, then beating a drum. "Warriors help me get my sick men to Plimoth."

"The Plimoth soldiers was to start marching home after they knew their man, Alden, had sailed." Red Nose spoke in a rush, but I knew he understood we needed to find San-dish. He called to a young fellow with only a few scraggly hairs on his chin. "Git goin' and tell the Plimoth soldiers to help us git these savages outta here." Scraggly Chin threw me a look that threatened to destroy my last remnants of dignity, but Red Nose clapped him on the head and he ran off.

Papa's chest barely moved. Turning my attention to my husband, I held his head up and touched the muscle in his cheek to open his jaw. His eyes opened, too, and he seemed to look at me. My hands trembling with fear and hope, I held the watercress mixture cup to his mouth. I stroked his throat to make him swallow, and finally he got some down.

Turning to my father, I tried to get some water into his mouth. It dribbled down his chin instead. My hope for Black Whale was tainted with the understanding that my father might soon be gone. Tears collected in my throat, and I swallowed hard. I would not cry now. My husband needed all my attention.

After repeated attempts, Black Whale was able to get most of the watercress drink down. He coughed fiercely and brought up some of the bad spirits in his chest. I'd asked the Strangers for seethed water and Red Nose now brought me a little pot. Putting the boneset to steep, I sat watching my men. Papa barely moved. I did not try to get any more liquid down his throat. Black Whale dozed a few minutes, then raised his head and drank some boneset. It would taste bitter, but he got enough down to cough up more. He slept again, as I watched his face anxiously, terrified he would slip away. "You must live," I told him over and over.

Nippa'uus was high when a white-cloth man called out the arrival of Plimoth warriors. With relief and apprehension, I rushed to the ladder to see Stephen Hopkins and two others. A bark startled me and I saw Hopkins' big dog, Sunny, a descendant of Rogue, the first Plimoth dog, and our own.

Hopkins came up the ladder, followed by the others and Scraggly Beard. They looked at me, but could not see my father and husband lying behind me

"Captain Standish sent me with two men to rescue the Indians but took the rest of his men back to Plimoth," Hopkins told Red Nose.

I turned my back on Hopkins and the others and felt my father's chest. It was rigid. *My father is dead,* repeated in my head. My father had helped the Strangers for many circles of the seasons. And now, others from their tribe had thrown him in the Big Salt Water and killed him.

Touching Papa's closed eyes lightly, I said the prayer for his journey. His spirit would not leave his body until he was buried properly.

"Hopamoch dead?" Hopkins asked with shock. The men bowed their heads in respect.

"We done what we could." Red Nose addressed his comments to Hopkins, who lowered his eyes.

"And thy husband?" Hopkins asked me.

"He is coughing. The remedy is working." I motioned drinking. "We can take him on my horse. I will sit behind him to hold him up." I paused, looking back at my father's body. We had to get him home. "Can you get a horse to carry my father's body?"

"We have to get out of Boston before dark. We have no time to secure a mount," Hopkins replied.

"Then we must use your dog and make a travois for my father's body."

At Hopkins' direction, Red Nose found a cloth to make a sling. The men used it to lower my father's body to the boards below, then put Black Whale in it and carefully lowered him. He groaned but did not cry out.

"Papa is gone," I whispered to my husband. "You are still young. Stay with me and our children."

I jumped on Mama's horse, sat behind the saddle and the men carefully boosted Black Whale up in front of me. "See what your people have done to my husband," I said. I tried to keep my voice even, but the bitterness showed.

"It was Boston men, not us," Hopkins said.

Yet I knew the Boston men were like some of the Plimoth men. And even Plimoth friends like Hopkins trusted us mainly because of the bounty they gained from us. The words of treaty provided for the trade which kept the Plimoth people friendly. Without the furs, fish, and trees that they took from us and sent to their people across the Big Salt Water, we would be viewed as if we were scum, like they viewed the Narragansett and the Massachuseuk.

I pushed these thoughts away and turned my attention to Black Whale, slumped against me. I hung onto Black Whale with my arms and held onto my horse with my thighs. Let him survive, I prayed, until I get him home so Mama can heal him.

The realization that I was delivering my father's body to my mother suddenly shook me.

14

Elisabeth:

The storm continued to lash at our fort. I could only hope John and our son were safely protected somewhere. The sky was so dark that I lit candles, but the wind coming through the chinks of our walls made the flames dance, so I blew them out and built up the hearth fire instead. I gathered my daughters around me and began telling them stories and singing songs.

After leading them in prayers, I laid my daughters on their bedding on the floor. Taking Baby Lydia, I crawled into our bed, but did not close the bed curtains. As I said my own prayers, I chided myself for worrying. Poor Priscilla, with her husband a week's travel away in a dangerous place and I had advised her to believe in the best but failed to take my own advice.

The door banged open and I sat up. A shape in the door told me it was not the wind. My husband shrugged out of his jacket and held me.

"Elisa."

"Jack." It seemed a long time since we'd called each other the pet names we'd used when we first fell in love. I leaned into his damp but warm body. Then my head cleared.

"Where's young John?"

"He's fine. He's with Priscilla."

"With Priscilla? Why? Is he all right? What took thee so long?"

John picked up the rough towel hanging from a peg above the bed.

"It's a long tale," he said.

"Then tell it," I replied, with a querulous tone. A small twist of jealousy lodged in my chest. But why was my husband taking care of John Alden's household instead of his own? I knew Priscilla needed assistance, but night had fallen at least an hour ago. What kind of assistance did she need? John stroked my arm and took my hand. I did not respond to his touch, nor did I push him away.

"Young John and I had finished chores and stopped at the bunkroom," John began. "We got to talking about Moses Talbot with the men." He swallowed hard. There had not been much talk about our friend since his murder. "I stopped at Priscilla's rooms to make sure her shutters were closed tight." He got up and poured some water from the bucket. A sudden bolt of lightning illuminated him and shook the fort. John brought water to me and I took a sip.

"Then what?"

"A large tree got hit by lightning—or knocked down by the wind. It fell so close to Alden's rooms that I feared it might hit the roof."

"But it missed?"

"Yea, but not by much. I went downstairs to try the door. The wind was so strong I could hardly open it, and the tree lay so near that it scraped against the door." He paused. "It was raining hard and the wind blowing trees around."

"And young John?" I asked.

"Priscilla let him bed down with her boys while I checked on things, and he's still asleep."

"And what have ye been doing?" I held my breath.

"Me? Well, I came back here, didn't I?" In the dark I could not see his face nor could he see mine. Surely mine would not be a pleasant sight what with everything going through my head. He stripped off his stockings and pulled at his laces. "Help me with the points," he said.

I did not respond and he turned to look at me. "Surely ye don't think...?"

I felt like I was a very young maid who did not know her man. My memory of watching Moses Talbot's young frame gave me a taste of my own medicine. Attraction is not easily resisted. Was God punishing me for my thoughts? Moses died and now I was suspicious of my husband.

John turned away so I could reach his points. I loosened them and he pulled off his breeks and then turned back to kiss me. "Ye needn't worry," he said.

I was ashamed of my childish jealousy, but it was not necessary to reveal it to John. Even when Moses Talbot seemed attractive to me, I would never have made room in my heart for anyone but John. I should be as confident of my husband as I expected him to be of me. Finding a dry nightshirt in the trunk, I helped him put it on, then we both got into bed. If only John Alden would return, Priscilla would have her husband back in her bed.

JUNE 1634
MOONE'S QUANI-MUC, HILL THE WEACHIMIN MOON

Attitash:

Later, when I tried to remember delivering my father's body to Mama, I could recall nothing except her wail. It filled the air around us, it went to the sky and out to the Big Salt Water. It seemed to last longer than the fading light going behind the western hills.

We chanted the mourning prayer as we covered Papa's body with red ochre and wrapped him in soft skins. I was so exhausted I fell asleep right along with my children. Black Whale slept fitfully beside me and I woke with him several times during the night.

The journey to our home village, Paomet, was a blur. Fish Hawk rode first, leading Papa's horse which carried his shrouded body, as Mama, with Mosk's arms around her, followed behind on her horse, watching over Papa. My sister, White Flower, had her baby in the cradleboard, as I did mine. Black Whale rode his own horse. I tried not to hover beside him, especially when he swayed backward instead of sitting forward toward the horse's neck. My sister's husband watched us all from the end of the line.

Our Massasoit and the Grandmothers' Caucus led the days' long ceremonies of prayers, songs, dancing, and wailing, until finally, Papa's body was lowered into his grave, covered by mats, and then covered with earth.

ON THE TRIP FROM Paomet back to Plimoth, each step seemed to follow in Papa's footprints to the Spirit-world. When we arrived in Plimoth, the Brewsters,' Bad-fords' and Hopkins' came to our homesite to give their sympathy and respects. They told us that when Edward Win-sow returned from across the Big Salt Water, he would be "most sorrowful." They did not mention Jon-owland and Esapett.

Elisabeth:

The corn we planted was already up to our knees when one evening, just after sundown, I heard shrieks from outside my open window. The cries forced an echo in my body. We all ran downstairs and outside. The shallop was in view! Through the gloaming light, we could finally make out the figures of John Alden and William Latham.

My John grabbed my hand and we ran to the riverbank. Priscilla fell onto the ground in tears and stayed there until the shallop had landed and her husband took her in his arms.

Once Priscilla and the children at last released John Alden from their embrace, we all sat down together in the Koussinoc great room and heard the chilling tale of his imprisonment and final release.

Long after dark, when all the children were asleep, John held me in a tight embrace, still angry from what had befallen him and his men. "I am not a murderer, but if I were faced with Moses' killer again I would not hesitate to shoot."

I stroked his face. "I know thee to be a man who would only kill to defend us."

When John was asleep, a question wound its way from a long-hidden place in my mind. *How had Squanto died?* Had Attitash and I poisoned him or did God take him? At the time, King Massasoit and Governor Bradford agreed Squanto had died of bad spirits—plague, small poxe, or any number of diseases. Attitash and I could not tell whether the poison we'd given Master Hopkins to serve Squanto had worked or if the Lord had taken him His own way. Tucked away in my heart, the question of blood on mine own hands still lingered.

Autumn, Pohquitagunkeeswush

Attitash:

During our Plimoth friends' harvest celebration, Mama and I told Bad-ford that we could no longer stay with them. "We will go back to Paomet to live. Our Massasoit will choose someone else to live here at Plimoth to ensure your people keep our treaty."

Bad-ford and their new sachem, Prence looked at us as if they did not understand.

"Why not? You are our friends…" Bad-ford said.

"Ahhe, friends who live with Our Massasoit," Mama said.

"Black Whale will take Hopamoch's role," Bad-ford said, as if saying it made it so.

"You heard what my wife's mother said," he told Bad-ford. "Someone else will come."

"When Jon-owland and Esapett return, will you tell them we will come visit?" I asked.

"Howland? The man in Kennebec?" Sachem Prence asked. "The one involved in the Boston situation?"

"Yea, Howland leads the group there," Bad-ford told the sachem. "John Alden has returned to Koussinoc and all is smooth now."

I was relieved to hear that but wondered if that meant Esapett and Jon-owland would not come back to Plimoth. My own life demanded that I not worry about someone so far away. Esapett would return or she would not. Either way, I had a husband to heal, a father to mourn, children to raise, and my people to save from her people.

Elisabeth:

Attitash and Black Whale had been gone from Plimoth for a year when Seafoam appeared to me in my dream. I had been sitting in my room when she entered and, before I could speak, said "You thought I was lost. But I need my daughter. I need Red Berry."

Breathing fast, I replied, "But she's not here! Attitash took her home."

"I know that, Attitash took her to my mother. But I need her now."

Her words made no sense, but dreams are not always logical.

I then noticed a man's hand gripping Seafoam's shoulder. His face was turned away. I thought it might be her first husband, Shimmering Fish, but when he turned toward me my body filled with spasms. Squanto spoke in a harsh whisper. "I want Seafoam's daughter. Bring her or I will come again."

A tugging on my nightcap felt as if Red Berry was with me, but as my mind released the dream, I knew it was my own babe, Lydia. My limbs ached and I feared falling into the dream again. I moved into my husband's arms and he responded by enclosing me. Not wanting to be questioned, I tried to breathe the deep, slow, sleep-breath. It worked. John asked no questions, his own breath like mine.

The dream was still with me when I woke up in the morning. I shoved it down and went about my day. After supper, John and I went down to the great room for a pipe and conversation. It being early May, the sun was still above the hill and the children were playing outside.

I took up my little white clay pipe. When I first married, I used a pipe to look like an upgrown woman. Now I enjoyed the calm spirits the pipe gave me. After I had a smoke with Priscilla, I went to where the men were gathered and took my husband by the hand. "Come look at the moon."

John was accustomed to my whims, so he nodded to the men and went outside with me.

We walked toward the river, its rush of melting spring water roaring past. The white moon hung high, waiting to shine when the golden sun upriver sank toward the hills. I leaned into him, then turned so I could see his face. "I had a bad dream last night."

He did not look concerned. "What this time?"

"I dreamed about Squanto."

John's face changed, the small furrow between his eyes deepened. "God's teeth! Why would ye dream about him after all these years? Ye were just a girl when he died."

But I was fourteen then, I thought—long past age seven, when children become responsible. Squanto died without our knowing if he even drank the poison. I thought to remind my husband now about that dreadful time, but knew he would never forget, so told him my dream. "Red Berry was in the dream too," I said. "Squanto was looking for her—he said Seafoam needed her."

John gripped my arms. "Wash the dream from thy mind. It could be Squanto trying to haunt thee. This is long over—Squanto and Seafoam are both gone." John felt my tremble. "Do not fear, God is with thee. And so am I."

I tried to do as John told me and wash the dream away. The next morning I woke up at first light—in spring this was before anyone else was awake. We had a corner room and I could see both the ring of light in the east and, turning a little, catch the heavy moon sinking in the west. My prayer for cleansing the dream was fervent and as I prayed I remembered when Attitash's mother had washed me gently while singing prayers to her Wampanoag God. I pushed up my nightdress sleeves and ladled water slowly over my arms, the bowl catching what didn't soak in. I prayed silently, not to awaken my family.

Crawling back into bed, I spooned into my husband, praying God would deal with Squanto's ghost before he got to me again. His death must be forgotten—it could not continue to torment me and my family. As my husband told me, I was very young that first tumultuous year. Trying to poison Squanto was far and away the worst of all the sins I'd committed then—both doing what I should not have done and not doing what I should have done. I kept my old sin tucked away.

We were busy preparing to move back home to Plimoth. Negotiations with the Abenaki were friendly. The fort would be maintained by someone else from Plimoth—someone without five children and another on the way. God would be with me. I had to believe that.

15

Attitash:

Black Whale and I had been home in Paomet a full change of seasons when Esapett and Jon-owland came back to Plimoth. It was so comfortable with our family—no Strangers stirring up our calm waters—that neither Black Whale nor I was in a rush to leave and go visit them.

Esapett might ask me to bring Red Berry for a visit and that might not be easy for Red Berry. She was thriving with her clan relatives, I assured myself. Red Berry's eyes were almost golden. Her hair was light brown, with a little reddish cast to it. Would Esapett comment on her appearance?

My brother, Fish Hawk, now lived at Plimoth, acting as Papa had done to keep the treaty our Massasoit and Bad-ford had signed after the Strangers arrived seventeen years ago.

Fish Hawk came home with word that Esapett was due to deliver another child, her sixth! I did not dream about Esapett, but I felt her restless spirit when I was awake or asleep. Maybe this baby would not be born easily. Pepe'warr moon would soon bring frost. If I wanted to travel to Plimoth, I should do it before the snow came. When my brother returned to Plimoth, I went along.

Elisabeth:

I seldom left our new house. I no longer rode a horse, not wanting to shake the baby out too early. John took the ox cart to haul in the harvest, but that was bouncy and most uncomfortable. I was busy with my children and drying all the vegetables from the garden, so I was content to stay at home in Rocky Nook when John went into Plimoth.

However, as my time drew nigh, I grew restless and decided to walk to the spring and little waterfall. Although I relished the sight and sound of the water, I seldom came, as Squanto's presence there at his death might still taint the place. However, it was the only waterfall close enough to walk to in my condition.

A crack of branch startled me. Looking up, I saw someone walking toward me. Attitash! I rose hastily, holding my belly, and lurched toward her. My babe kicked against Attitash while we held each other in a long, tight hug. When we released each other, I felt as though someone was watching us.

She stepped back, looking into my eyes. "What's wrong?"

Instead of answering her, I looked at the boulders surrounding the waterfall. "Do ye not recognize this place?" When she did not answer, I whispered. "This is the place where they found Squanto's body."

"Ahhe. But that was a long time ago."

"Squanto hasn't forgotten," I told her. "He comes to me in a dream."

Attitash closed her eyes, her face quiet. "Your words catch in a web in my mind. I must think."

A shock of pain hit me. I grabbed my stomach and howled. Attitash held me when the pain continued to hold me in its claw. I tried to walk, but the babe was coming too fast. I couldn't move. Attitash took hold of my shoulders and helped me to lie down.

"You will bring your baby to the light here."

Not in this place, I thought. I should never have come here instead of staying at home. At least I had told my husband I might walk to the waterfall. He might wonder why I had not returned in good time.

Pain shut my throat, but my eyes must have shown my fear to Attitash.

"Do not worry, Esapett, I will keep the bad spirits away."

I had no strength to resist. Attitash laid her cloak down on some moss near the spring and helped me squat. Between my pains, she gathered dry reeds, pulling fluff out of cattails which she piled under me. I was scarcely aware of the smoke she blew over my face. It was pungent, but soothing.

Time dragged when the pains got worse, until time seemed to stop when a brief respite allowed me to sleep. Attitash massaged my back and got water from the spring to bathe my head.

As the pains got stronger, I panted so I would not deliver, but this babe would not wait. With one great surge of pain and energy, I pushed my child out. Attitash caught the babe. She slapped the babe on the back and a healthy cry assured me it breathed. Attitash showed me the babe's tiny bud between the legs. Another daughter. My fifth girl.

When she had wiped the babe with moss, Attitash tweaked my nipple and put the babe to my breast. At first, the babe only sniffed, but I knew how to pop her mouth open and slide my nipple in. She latched on and I drew a deep breath. Better a healthy daughter than a sick son. Attitash tied the cord with a string she drew from those wrapped on her arms, then reached into her bag for a small knife to cut the cord. She dipped her cloth in the spring and wiped my babe's face and hair.

I settled down on her cloak. I would have to wait for strength before I could walk. I hoped that would not be necessary—that my John would come to carry me back. This babe had come so fast, my husband and children would not be looking for me yet. I dozed off, then woke again, thinking of my daughter's open-air birth. I studied her pink cheeks and felt the strength of her suck. "I will call my babe, 'Hannah'," I told Attitash.

She raised her fine brows. "You give her a name already? You don't know her. We must watch her for three days. On the third day—her spirit day—you will give her a name."

"I don't need to wait three days. I know she's strong," I answered. "Hannah was a strong woman in our bible—our stories. A judge."

Attitash looked puzzled, but I hadn't the energy to explain what a judge was. I patted my new babe's cap of hair and sniffed it. It had a rosy cast. "Did ye get all the blood washed out?"

Attitash touched a soft strand nestled behind my babe's ear. "Ahhe, that's the color of her hair. The color of a baby fox."

"Orange?" My fearful chill returned to my neck. "Did a curse do this?"

Attitash:

While I gathered more sphagnum moss, Esapett chattered. "We are where Squanto's body was found. I saw him in my dreams." She stopped and breathed deeply, gathering her strength so she could talk. "Because we gave him enough black cohosh to kill him, I am guilty. Squanto cursed my babe and that made her hair red." Tears slid from her eyes as she cuddled her new baby. "God forgive me."

The brook's gurgling made more sense than Esapett. As I struggled for words to ease her confused fears, I wondered what kind of dream Tisquantum had appeared in. I was glad that he had never visited me. If I could tell Esapett's dream to Mama, she would understand what Esapett did not. Tisquantum was an enemy of our people—and a threat to the Strangers. I could only be glad he was gone. Knowing my words were useless, I stroked Baby Hannah's cheek.

"She sucks well," I told Esapett. "Your baby is strong. You're right. If Hannah means 'strong,' it is a good name for her."

Esapett closed her eyes and slept. She would need to gather strength if she had to walk home. Where were her daughters? Her husband? No one ready to bring her baby to the light should be out walking alone. If they did not come, I would have to carry her back myself.

To gather my own strength, I listened to the splash of the waterfall, birds murmuring, and wind rustling the trees. I watched the dark brown oak and red maple leaves languidly twist while the birch fluttered, delighted with the breeze. Above us, the sky was a solid blue bowl. One little cloud clung to the western rise of the hills. Nippa'uus shone at the top. A low snap alerted me to a doe stepping carefully to the water whirling beneath the falls. She raised her head and gazed at us a long moment, then lowered it to drink. As she stepped back, her fawn peeked out from the bushes, then both disappeared.

My breathing slowed. It felt like the tide ebbing back into the Big Salt Water. I relaxed, letting go of restless thoughts, and turned my heart to listen to Esapett's. Her breathing matched mine.

Esapett opened her eyes a moment. "My husband must be searching for me. Do ye think ye could go find him?"

I nodded my head in agreement to keep her quiet, but I would not leave her alone. She closed her eyes and slept again.

I sang a prayer that Jon-owland would know where we were and come find us. If only he could open his heart to his gods and listen to where we were! But the Stranger's prayers were not like ours. Fish Hawk said that Jon-owland spoke to him, as Esapett had to me, of praying to their god to take away 'guilt, sin,' and 'for-giveness.' We understood only that the Strangers used these words to describe something essential to their gods. These words seethe in their hearts like bad spirits in a neglected wound. I yearned to ease both Jon-ow-land and Esapett's hearts. I would sit with her now, until her husband came. If no one had come when Nippa'uus began to sink, then I would carry her home.

Taking my drowsy friend's hand, I held it lightly with my thumb on her wrist. Her blood pulsed strong. Esapett's chest rose and fell with my breaths. Baby Hannah's cheek molded to her mother's breast, her tiny lips smacking as the early al-most-milk dripped.

Having just been brought to light, the baby was as fresh as the water springing from the moss. This new daughter was not tainted with the soul-shriveling that her people struggled against.

I stroked Esapett's hands, one at a time, starting with the soft round below her thumb, then through her palm and up to the tips of her fingers. Her hands lost their limp yielding and responded by pressing back slightly.

I closed my eyes and slid into an almost-sleep. Esapett's low voice woke me. "Where is my husband? I am recovered enough to go home if he carries me."

"He must be on his way," I said. "Rest for now. If he is not here soon, I will carry you." But she would not close her eyes, insisting that her husband must be searching and would be afraid if he came to the waterfall and we were no longer here, so I agreed to go toward the main trail and call.

Esapett's eyes followed me as her baby happily sucked at her teat. I walked a short way and stopped to listen. I could feel the thud of horse hooves in the ground before I heard them. It was not long before the horse came into view and Jon-owland jumped off. "Have ye seen my wife?" When I nodded back toward the little waterfall, the worried knot be-tween his eyes disappeared. "Thank you, Attitash."

THREE MORNINGS LATER, on Baby Hannah's spirit day, I wait-ed until Esapett had eaten her eggs and bread and then drank her tea before I told her I'd be leaving soon to go to my people in Paomet. "I wanted to come to see how you are. Now that I know, I will go home," I told her.

She looked up at me with hurt in her eyes. "But not already! Ye just came. And it takes thee four hours to walk back."

Before I came to see Esapett, I knew I would have to explain why we no longer could be with each other as we used to be, even if we could trust them to keep secret Black Whale's having the firestick. My words had been gathering in my head ever since we returned from Koussinoc. "Netop—Friend, it is not the same here in Plimoth as when we all lived here. Many, many more of your people here. Many more Strangers."

"It is true that we have an increase in population, but not nearly the growth Boston realized," Esapett said.

I started to interrupt, to tell her to drop the fancy words she was using—just like Bad-ford, Win-slow, and the new Strangers use—but Esapett pushed more words at me and I closed my mouth.

"Ye don't need to go to Plimoth," she insisted. "Stay here at Rocky Nook with us."

She did not understand I was not speaking of only her family and mine. "This place is now yours," I told her. "Like all this land at Patuxet is now yours."

It had been years since I'd used our Wampanoag name for Plimoth. Esapett tried to say "Pa-tu-xet?" then said, "But you are always welcome here! You, Black Whale, thy children."

I spread my arms out to encompass the view from her yard. "All this you call Rocky Nook. The trees you cut down to plant, the streams, the waterfalls...they were all Wampanoag. They were our People's."

Tears gathered in her eyes. I turned to see Fish Hawk and Mosk as they arrived at Howland's door, accompanied by Jonowland and their son.

"Look who's here," son Jon said to his mother. The boy was born when my Mosk was four. He looked up to Mosk and Fish Hawk, who were taller than his father. Jon-owland invited my brother and son to sit. They greeted Esapett with eyes lowered. Esapett told her daughter to pour tea for the men as I gathered my few belongings in a pack.

"Mosk went on his vision quest, he will soon have his coming of age ceremony," Fish Hawk said. I tried to catch his eye—no need to get into a long story our friends would not understand. But Jon-owland and their son were full of questions—where did he go on the vision quest? Who was with him? Was it safe? My brother brushed them off with a laugh, however.

"It's too long a story. And it's Mosk's story. I can tell you after Mosk goes back to Paomet." Fish Hawk reminded our friends that he was living at our homesite near Plimoth now and they would have time for stories.

Esapett started to ask a question, or seemed to, before she had a change of mind. Esapett and I embraced lightly. There was reluctance in our gesture as we said our goodbyes.

As my son and I left, we heard young Jon asking when he would be taken to Paomet. We began our walk back to our family, our own people.

April 1638
Rocky Nook

Elisabeth:

"Look, Mother, Hannah can sit up by herself," my daughter Hope called.

A big smile lit my babe's face as she wobbled slightly. It was a beautiful spring evening, the sun already low over the western hills. I was taking an after-supper break. My oldest girl and her younger sister were washing up in the kitchen, my husband and son were carrying in the last of the firewood for an evening fire. They turned at Hope's call, just in time to see Hannah topple over. She whimpered until Hope picked her up. Hope took the babe's bonnet off and ran her fingers through the soft, orange-red curls.

"Does Hannah's hair come from fire?" Hope asked me. "That's what Johnny says." She stuck her tongue out at her big brother.

Young John shot a superior look at Hope. "I said it was the color of fire, Miss Know-it-all. But wouldn't it be fun if..."

"Enough!" I scolded.

I'd not mentioned our babe's hair since her birth in the woods. Attitash's calm response at her birth had quelled my fears. However, without Attitash to reassure me, as the babe grew and her hair thickened to a bright color, my fears returned. I hesitated to tell John that I still wondered if our daughter's red hair was retribution from Squanto's ghost.

"Take the babe in and change her clout," I now told Hope. "I'll be in soon to nurse her to sleep. John, go with thy sisters. There's some corn cake in the keep-cupboard. Help yourselves and tell Desire and Elizabeth they can have some and give a bite to Lydia."

My husband sat down beside me on the bench outside our house. It gave us a good view of the bay that reflected the sun. We sat in silence for a minute, then he asked, "What's going on?"

"Her brother and sisters tease Hannah about her red hair," I told him. "But as she grows, other children will tease her, too. Someone will say it's a curse."

John's brows knit together. "Why do ye think there's a curse? Surely our child's hair color is no such sign." When I only leaned against him in silence, he continued. "Mayhap ye look for a sign because of my guilt."

"Thy guilt!" I sat up to look him in the face. "What else could have been done? Hocking started it and would have killed more if he had not been shot. Hocking deserved to die."

John took my face in his hands. "Of course he did, and I

bear neither guilt nor regret for his death." John put his arms around me again. "Nay, it's not Hocking's death. It's Talbot's. I live with the burden of Moses Talbot's death."

"But Hocking killed Talbot! Why should ye feel guilty?"

"I was in charge. I neglected to perceive the threat Hocking posed. Two men were killed because I did not protect my men from danger." John took my hand, and the tension in his body shot through our grip.

"There is blood on my hands, too," I whispered. When he turned to me in disbelief, I blurted out, "Ye must remember that Attitash and I conspired to kill Squanto. We wanted a plant that would be lethal if taken in a large dose, but not draw attention. That's why we used black cohosh—a remedy for female troubles that could kill in large doses."

John opened his mouth, then closed it again. "But ye did not poison Squanto thyself. That's why I made thee give the dose to Stephen Hopkins. I recall our discussion over the danger of thy carrying it to Hopkins thyself and I made Stephen come to our house."

"Yea, Master Hopkins served Squanto the large dose of black cohosh in strong drink."

"So why do ye still worry that Attitash and ye were the cause of his death?" he asked, his voice thick with dismay.

"Attitash and I plotted the whole thing. Master Hopkins did what we asked. When Squanto was found dead a few days later, I hoped it was part of God's plan for our people and not Satan's. But I've never known for sure."

John dropped my hand and took hold of my shoulders. "Ye did this when only a young woman. Why should ye worry about it now?"

"No one knows how Squanto died." I repeated. "Maybe we killed him, maybe there was not enough black cohosh and he died by other means."

"God took him—whatever means killed him. He was an enemy to King Massasoit as well as our enemy. As for talk of a curse," John took my left hand and held it up in front of us. "Thy mother said this hand is cursed. That thy left hand was controlled by Satan. Do ye still believe that?"

I looked at my hand, no longer a young girl's hand. Along with my wedding ring, came muscle, bigger knuckles and visible veins. "Nay, I believe this hand is just more useful than my right."

"Then why do ye believe our daughter's hair color is a curse?"

"Well, everyone knows it's a curse." I kept my voice calm, but it irritated me when John questioned me. "And that terrible Goodman Billington had red hair and he was finally hanged for murder."

"Stop!" John put his hand to my mouth. I tried to quell my anger, but still did not speak.

We were both quiet for a long minute. "We will not tell our children about Squanto," I finally said.

"Yea, we will not." John folded me in his arms. "No one really knows who killed Squanto, nor does anyone know who killed Hocking. I was not the only one with a gun." John released me from his embrace. Keeping his silence, he looked down at his hands. "Elisabeth, I wish I could tell thee." Looking up at me, his eyes had turned from deep moss green to bright, a sure sign he was reaching deep inside himself.

"Must ye keep a secret?" My mind raced from one possibility to another. "Ye are the one who shot Hocking?"

"Nay. I don't know that I shot him. Or yea. I don't know if I killed him." He gripped my hands in his. "But I wish I had! I could atone for the loss of Moses Talbot." He paused again as I crammed down the many questions I had, most of which were the names of the men with John in that boat.

John let go of my hands, leaving me to clench them in my lap. He stood and paced and then returned to sit by me. "The only way to prevent my ever being hanged is to figure out the one who killed him. But with so many guns being fired, this would be impossible.

"Why would anyone be hanged? It was in defense of everyone in that boat. In defense of all of us!"

"John Alden was not even with us in the boat when Hocking was shot, but he spent a month in Boston jail. Governor Prence is controlled by the greedy men who backed the poaching. They would demand a hanging if they knew who did it!" John's eyes tightened, as if to ward off the sight of a friend dangling from a rope.

"Don't ye trust me?" I drew myself up. "I'm a grown woman with six children. I can keep a secret!"

John gently put his arm around me. "Of course, I trust thee. But I have no secret knowledge to tell thee."

I remembered handing the bundle from Fish Hawk to John, the gun he'd given Black Whale. But Black Whale was not in the boat. I would never know if he used the gun.

"So we live with no answers," I said. "Ye will wonder if ye could have prevented Moses' murder. I will continue to wonder if I played God when Attitash and I gave Squanto poison." My pent-up fear nearly choked me and I drew a deep breath. "God knows not one of His children is innocent." I wept in his arms, until my tears washed my heart.

16

Attitash:

I waited until the harvest was in to go to Rocky Nook to see Esapett. The spirits favored the weather and crops, making it a good time to journey. Black Whale stayed home to hunt while the stags were rutting. I brought the children with me.

It was Mosk's first time as the man protecting us on a journey since his coming of age. He'd earned the right during the summer on his vision quest. Now, Mosk walked ahead of me, carrying his bow and arrow. When we arrived at Rocky Nook, young Jon-owland and Mosk went to the meadow where Mosk could show his friend how to shoot with bow and arrow.

Esapett and I both carried new life, the bumps in our bellies just showing. Her little Hannah was toddling about, her fire-colored hair curled about her head. Red Berry's hair was close to the color of Hannah's. Would Esapett's next baby have hair the color of fire, too? Esapett warned me not to take Red Berry into Plimoth. "Some people there call children with hair this color 'cursed,' possessed by what you call, 'bad spirits,' she told me.

When our sons came back from what Esapett called "arms practice," both young men were excited. "We're going to ask Jon-owland if he can teach us how to use his pistol."

My heart lurched. We'd never told Mosk that his father had fired Jon-owland's firestick while we were at Koussinoc. Esapett's stricken face matched mine.

"We can't use guns," I said. Hearing the tone in my voice, Mosk did not object. Esapett took her son aside and obviously told him something he'd not known.

It drained some of the pleasure out of our reunion.

MAY 1649

Elisabeth:

The moon was just rising from the eastern edge of the sea, its glow reached to the western woods and mingled with the last rays of the setting sun. John and I stood at the window, looking west. He pulled me against him and bent his head, his mouth close to my ear.

Should I tell him now or would it ruin the beauty of the moment? John deserved to know, but I had not found the right time to tell him. With our children constantly around, there was little opportunity for private conversation. But now, our youngest, Ruthie, was tucked into her trundle bed and our older children were off playing.

"Look to the woods. See the owl?" John's arms tightened around me. "In the trees."

I saw nothing but moon glow and the first faint stars above the forest until a slight movement caught my eye. "It's huge. What is it?"

"It's a great gray owl."

We stood motionless. The only sound through the open window was the tide washing ashore. With a faint rustle, the owl lifted into the sunset, its huge wings pushing it slowly above the trees. We both laughed from the sheer beauty of its silent power.

When I could find my voice again, I spoke without considering how to broach the subject. "Ye know that our little Ruthie has been weaned some months now."

"Yea, she is thriving without thy milk." His response came softly. "And yet thy monthly courses have not returned."

I was surprised that he'd noticed. When our first child was born, twenty-five years ago, my husband had not paid attention to when my courses came. Nine children had taught him to notice. However, John might not have thought it necessary to pay attention to my monthlies now that I was a grandmother several times over. Thankfully, John's attentions were not limited to grandfatherly actions. Perhaps my husband was as relieved as I was to see the end of my childbearing years. John knew every childbirth to be a time of terror. "We have enough children," I said, assuming he'd agree.

John drew his arms tighter about me. "Well, ye are almost forty-two, ye are young enough to bear one more child."

The shock of his thought that I could be with child stopped me for a moment. The pride in John's voice told me that he relished the thought that he could still plant his seed. Well, he would know in a month or two. Let him dream. He would have to accept that nine children were sufficient for any man's legacy.

John kissed my neck with the assumption of a man long married. "If God spares me until I'm seventy-eight, little Ruthie would have a father when she is twenty and gets married. And if I live to be eighty, another child would also be twenty."

So he really was convinced that I could bear a child and he would live another twenty or so years. "Have ye not always said ye would live to be 80?" I asked.

"Yea, I said so. Until the incident in Maine."

Attitash:

My new granddaughter faced me from her mother's back, laced up and swathed, her features in dark shadows under the cradleboard's hood.

Crraaaack, boom, shattered the still air. My granddaughter wailed. I clamped my teeth so I would not wail, too.

My daughter Nipi brought the baby's cradleboard to the front and crouched down. I squat-crawled to them and we moved into the thick bushes. After all those circles of the seasons, the memory returned of hot pain when a Stranger's firestick assaulted my body killing my first baby before she was born. I pushed away that memory, but in its place came the reminder of the awful fear that gripped us all when we lived in Abenaki territory. The firesticks that boomed were enemy not only to us, but to Jon-owland.

I listened for silence—the absence of the firesticks and the only sound was the wings of an eagle spiraling toward us: flap, flap, flap, flap, glide; flap flap, flap, flap, glide, until she disappeared across the western trees. The air ruffed my cheeks and eyes, and I saw wind in the trees, waving and rubbing branches. A flurry of stuttering wings startled me, but the grouse flew up quickly and disappeared. We stayed huddled in the bushes but heard no more gunshot.

"Do you think that was the Strangers hunting, Mama?" Nipi knew that while only Strangers were allowed to use firesticks, some of our hunters still had guns secretly hidden. Not long before Nipi was born, new Cloth-men arrived in large numbers to steal our land. The new Strangers were full of fear and had no recognition that our People lived in this land many, many generations before they came. None of the People of our Land—Wampanoag, Abenaki, and Narragansett—were able to possess firesticks. Instead, most of our men continued to use our weapons to hunt—bow, arrow, and clubs. However, Nipi knew that some of our hunters took the firesticks out of hiding and practiced shooting so they would remember how to use them when they were needed to defend ourselves.

I did not answer her questions, keeping my finger on my mouth and hoping the baby stayed quiet. The firestick boomed again, farther away this time. We waited until we saw the eagle again, then we stood up and went back to the trail, searching for the hunters' footprints among the deer hooves.

"It should be safe to go down the slope to the water-cress spring. Whoever is shooting, they are out of range now," I told Nipi. We went slowly down the path. The blackberry canes wrapped around each other and snagged our dresses. When we reached the spring, Nipi put down the cradleboard and scooped the first handful of watercress. Her baby peeked out, black eyes big as a little owl's. As we gathered the tiny plants, we put them in the skin bag, keeping one eye on the cress and the other on the baby.

A scrunch of footsteps alerted me. I looked up to see my brother, Fish Hawk, with a young Stranger. As they came closer, I recognized our friends' son, young Jon-owland. Fish Hawk was in the lead, a bow over his shoulder and a plump turkey hanging from his belt. Young Jon-owland followed, a bow and quiver of arrows slung over his shoulder and a small firestick hanging from his side.

"Who fired the shot we heard?" I asked.

My brother shrugged. "Maybe Jon-owland is out hunting."

"Did you need a firestick to catch that slow turkey, Uncle Fish Hawk?" Nipi teased her clan uncle. Fish Hawk chuckled, "My snare took care of that." He turned to me, "We've not seen Black Whale. Do you know where your husband is?"

I laughed. "Once he leaves in the morning, I never know where his hunting and fishing take him. But I know he only took his bow today."

Young Jon-owland kept his eyes lowered to respect me, a grandmother. "Do all the honored Pniese hunt only with a bow and not a snare?"

"They use what they need," I answered.

"My uncle has given you a good bow." Nipi spoke to young Jon-owland firmly. "When you know how to use your bow and arrow, you will want it for all your prey." Nipi knew from our Moon Lodge story that I was once the prey and her older sister had died in my womb.

Elisabeth:

The morning after witnessing the owl's flight, I woke encased in John's arms. The house was quiet. My mind returned to our conversation about my husband surviving the Maine incident. It had stayed with me as we slept, with a strange dream that I was back in Maine, looking for my John to come home and yet other men kept arriving instead.

"I do not know God's will for my time on Earth, even though He has given me more than one escape from death," John had told me.

Now I asked, "Did ye wonder if all the escapes were used up fifteen years ago, when those poachers in Maine invaded our territory?"

John did not answer for a moment, then said softly "Yea, I feared 'twas the end of my earthly time."

Stroking his arm muscles, I marveled that despite his years, my husband felt even stronger than when we married years ago. I shifted in his arms so I could see his face. "Do ye mind that I'm not able to have any more babes?"

He opened his eyes and laughed softly.

"Why are ye laughing?" I whispered.

"I just remembered. When Mistress Brewster died, her husband told me their last son was born after she thought she had gone through the change."

"That's not funny." I bristled. "She was a dear lady and I miss her."

"We all do, but that's not why I'm laughing."

I sat up, pushing a curl back into my nightcap. "Then why?"

John gave me a long look, leaning to brush my breasts lightly. "Elisabeth, ye may be like Mistress Brewster."

I sat up, protesting his assumption. "I know my body! And I don't know how old Mistress was..." I stopped myself and reviewed my so-called signs of the change of life. Missing courses was not sufficient evidence. Was I ignoring signs of being with child? 'Twas true that my nipples were tender.

"Thy breasts are swelling," John traced the curve of one breast. "There's a glow about thee." His hand moved to cup my belly. "Feel the tightness? This bump is not padding, it's new life. I think we're going to have ten children. A chance for a fourth son, or a seventh daughter."

A small wail escaped and I did not try to stop the tears, still protesting that I was right and he was wrong.

John waited for me to stop blubbering. "Listen to thy body, Dear Heart. Maybe I'm wrong, but I think God has blessed us again."

I listened. A quiver filled me as I recognized the sense deep within me of a budding life. More tears flowed, as John embraced me.

"Why do ye not rejoice?" he asked.

I wiped my eyes and drew a deep breath. "Maybe I would not survive."

John stroked my cheek and traced my mouth with his finger. "Surely God did not spare me that day in Maine only to allow fifteen years later that childbed would take my wife and the mother of our children."

JULY 1649

The July heat sapped my energy. Anyone who looked at my belly knew that I carried another child. I had also been five months gone when we moved to Maine seventeen years ago. No matter the heat then, I'd felt strong. Having delivered four healthy children then, and being in my twenties, I was not assailed with doubts about childbed. I knew that travail was simply the pain of pushing out a little babe and it brought great joy. My only concern then was whether I'd ever give my husband a second son. Now, I'd delivered nine healthy children, including three sons. My worries about childbed and children should have been over.

A breeze from the west cooled my face. After all the trauma in Maine, I'd earned the blessed life we enjoyed in our new home at Rocky Nook. I put down the pan of beans I was snapping and stood to get a drink of water. *You've blessed me, Lord. Let this one be healthy and let it be the last.* Being grateful for my children and grandchildren did not wash away my fear.

It was just a few weeks ago, that the seed of this fear had taken hold. John had come home hastily to tell me he was going to the Bishope home, "on business." I thought mayhap Richard Bishope and his wife, Allis, had contested a bit of land. As magistrate, John was often called to settle such disputes. Allis Bishope often complained to me that she did not think her husband stood up for himself and that they deserved more. I believed that Allis's complaints derived from the sad lot she'd been dealt when her child was born with a stain of Satan on her face. Any mother with such heartbreak would naturally want to gain something else in life to compensate.

Shortly after my John left, our youngest son, four-year-old Jabez, came running. "Mother, everyone is going to Bishope's house. Why did Father go there?"

"What are ye talking about, Jabez?" I pushed his red hair from his forehead. His green eyes were wide with excitement. Jabez was only four, but he paid attention to everything.
"Come with me, Mother." Jabez took my hand, then looked at his sisters, gathered about the wash tub. "Hannah, stay with Ruthie."

Hannah rolled her eyes at me. "Why should a four-year-old boy boss a fourteen-year-old sister? It's bad enough when

Joseph tries to boss me." Joseph, nine years old now, seldom tried to rule her. Hannah sullenly dropped her laundry stick and sat by her little sister on the grass.

Governor Bradford waved back the people gathered at Bishope's home. "Your husband is inside," he said to me. "Go help."

"Get home and help Hannah," I told Jabez. He dared not protest. I made sure he was on his way, then went toward the house. Richard Bishope sat on the bench by the open door. He stared with wide eyes that did not see me or anyone else. I dared not speak to him but came close enough to see the absolute stillness of his face. He looked more like a carved figure than a man, as he whispered, "Dead."

I looked to William Bradford. "His wife?"

"Nay," our governor responded.

Richard Bishope looked at me for the first time. "Get Allis," he said.

"Where is she?" I raised my hands in question, but Goodman Bishope's eyes had gone blank again.

"There's a mess to clean up." Governor Bradford called to the women standing in a horrified clutch. "Bring water and cloths."

The door behind Richard Bishope was still open. I stepped inside. Allis wasn't dead, as I assumed, but stood rooted just inside the door. Her feet were steady on the floor, but her body bent forward as though she bore a large bundle on her back. Her shoulders and dress were a crimson-splattered apron of blood. She raised her head and her eyes roved wildly from one corner to the other. She trembled as though Satan possessed her, as he obviously did. Her husband did not turn to look at her. She stumbled toward me, then halted on the doorstep.

"Devil took Daughter back where she came from," she spat out. Goodman Bishope twitched as though his wife had lashed him, but still refused to look at her.

I took hold of Allis's shoulders to steady her, but held her at arm's length. Francis Cooke came from the house to lead her away, saying "You come with me to the holding cell." She did not resist.

Wondering where my husband was, I stepped back into the house. A dark blot of blood pooled at the foot of the ladder. The puddle looked freakishly like the stain that had covered the Bishope daughter's cheek since birth—as if the devil had removed his mark from the child's face and spilled it on the floor. I put a fist into my belly to stop its roiling. At the sound of footsteps, I looked up the ladder to see my husband descending.

"What did ye find?" I asked with what breath I could muster.

John looked back over his shoulder as he reached the floor. His green eyes flashed like clouds rumbling with storms. "Get out, Elisabeth. 'Tis a vile place!" John's voice shook with anger.

I backed up, the clench in my throat stopped any words. I fled home, oblivious to the gawking crowd.

When John returned home, an hour or so later, his face was scarcely more animated than Richard Bishope's. Without a word, he gathered our children into his arms. I had been trying to collect my wits sufficiently to speak to them, but failed to do anything but tell them to sit still and be quiet.

"Ye are all safe," John said slowly, as if he were explaining a complicated lesson to our children. "Goodwife Allis Bishope is possessed, and she's being held until her trial. There will be much gossip, but none of ye may speak of the murder."

I caught the look between Lydia and Hannah, as they mouthed "murder." Knowing they would talk about it to each other regardless, I said, "Do not speak of this murder to anyone outside our house."

John drew a deep breath. The knot between his eyes quivered from his effort to quell his anger. "Mother is right. You may speak only to each other."

"What murder?" Hannah asked.

Her father silenced her with a look. "We will tell thee in good time. Meanwhile, say only what needs be said."

"What about our sisters, Desire, Hope, and Elizabeth?" Lydia asked. "They live with their husbands and children."

"No need for thee to speak to thy sisters, Mother and I will talk to them." John picked up his bible and gathered the children to listen. I tried to sing to myself as I cleaned up supper, hoping to calm myself. The words of the lullaby Attitash taught me came from my mouth—though not my mind—until the last line. "Then down will come Baby, cradle and all." I choked back the words. When I'd warned Attitash not to take Red Berry into Plimoth, I had not imagined that someone would murder her own child to get rid of Satan. What would Allis Bishope have done to an Indian half-breed? Burned her at the stake?

John finished reading the bible to the children. I doubted the children heard his words, only the tears in his voice. With a wave of his hand, he sent them away. I saw to the younger ones' bedtime prayers. Their questions tumbled out, but I told them I knew nothing myself except what their father had already told them.

When I came down, John was sanding the ink on a paper. I drew some ale for him and took a beaker for myself. "I am forty-two years old, mother of nine, and a grandmother. Tell me what happened."

John looked at me, his mouth worked, but no words came out. He slammed his fist on his writing desk. "Why couldn't the blasted woman drown herself, instead of harming her child? She should have known!"

"We both heard the taunts," I interrupted. "Ever since the child was born, Allis has been accused of mating with Satan instead of her husband."

"Yea, but she should have ignored the kind of people who taunted her." John drew his hands over his smooth, handsome face.

"We saw her desperate attempts to stop them," I said. "Remember how Allis tried to conceal the stain by smearing mud over the stain on her daughter's face? And when that didn't work, she desperately tried various potions to make the purple stain disappear. She even held a candle close enough to cause a blister on the child's cheek."

"Did any of her friends try to stop her?" John asked me.

"What friends?" I could not pretend to my husband that I was her friend. "I learned not to allow our red-haired Hannah and Jabez near Allis—knowing she would call them cursed, to deflect attention from her own babe."

"Both of us know Allis Bishope is damned forever," John sighed, shoulders sagging with the knowledge.

"God alone knows where she'll spend eternity. We cannot know what compels a mother whose child carries Satan's mark," I tried to keep my hands still, but they knotted into each other. "But Allis may believe her child is released from Satan and is safe in God's arms."

The anger faded from John's eyes, leaving lines of anguish. "Governor has asked me to record what we found." He paused. "I put down the horrific details needed for her trial." A sob escaped him and I moved to sit by him and lean into his strong shoulder. "I will never rid the sight from my memory." He held one arm around me, his paper was face down on the table. "No one should see what we saw."

"It won't be in my eyes as it is in thine," I said softly, though I knew the pool of blood would always remain with me. "I must learn what ye've witnessed, John, or I will hear a slanted report from someone else."

"'Tis not easily read." John turned the paper over and I took it from his hands. "*These sheweth that on July the 22nd, 1648, wee whose names are underwritten were sworne by Mr. Bradford, Governor, to make inquiry of the death of the child of Allis Bishope, the wife of Richard Bishope. 'Wee declare coming into the house of the said Richard Bishope, wee saw at the foot of a ladder w'h leadeith into an upper chamber, much blood; and going up all of us into the chamber, wee found a woman child, of about foure years of age, lying in her shifts upon her left cheeke with her throat cut...and a bloody knife lying by the side of the child, with w'h knife all of us judged and the said Allis confessed to the few of us at one time, that shee murdered the child with the said knife."*

My eyes blurred with tears at the image of the poor child, the blood mark on her face and her own warm blood covering her throat and chest. I wiped my eyes and read the signatures. Twelve men witnessed: John Howland, James Hurst, Robert Lee, John Shawe, Francis Cook, John Cooke, James Cole, Gyells Richard, Richard Sparrow, Thomas Pope, Francis Billington, and William Nelson. The twelve witnesses agreed: Allis Bishope would be hanged.

What would I do if my new babe were to show a taint like the Bishope's babe?

I put the paper down, knelt by my chair, and prayed, "Lord, preserve us, our children and grandchildren." I paused, and whispered so my husband would not hear, "Lord, keep Satan from my womb!"

17

Attitash:

A picture stayed in my mind of the child's white throat, slit by her own mother. Fish Hawk told me of the tragedy when he came back from Plimoth a few sunrises after the child was killed. What or who possessed the child's murderous mother? I'd seen the little girl when she was just learning to walk. She wore a bonnet that could not conceal the dark red blotch spread over one white cheek. It could have signified her favor with the spirits, but Strangers in Plimoth insisted it was a curse. There was to be a trial.

I thanked our spirits that the child's mother had not attacked Hannah and Jabez, Esapett's children, for their hair was like fire as well. She might also have attacked our Red Berry for her light skin and reddish hair. Nipi and I agreed we would not let her baby, Little Breeze, near any of the Strangers' villages.

I rubbed my eyes to push away the image of the slain child and returned to my work. Bean vines were slowly climbing up the weachimin. The squash leaves surrounding the weachimin were big, filled with bright gold blossoms that promised us plenty of squash. Nipi's baby liked to stroke the flowers and put them in her mouth, coating her little lips with the gold dust. Nipi allowed Little Breeze to crawl through the soft earth where yesterday's rain had soaked into the ground. She was easy to have in the safety of our home in Paomet—as young mothers of seventeen summers usually are. Little Breeze tried to help us hoe the earth in piles around the weachimin plants. My bare feet enjoyed the same feeling that made my granddaughter wiggle her toes and clap her hands.

Nipi bent to her work for a few minutes, then paused. "Were you afraid of Strangers hurting me when I was a baby in Koussinoc?"

I put down my hoe and pulled my braids off my neck. "Ahhe, I had reason to be afraid of Strangers in Boston and other villages up north in what they call 'Maine,' but not of Esapett and Jon-owland. And though I was not close friends with the others—Pah-scilla and her Jon, I did not fear them."

Niki waited for me to say more. When I kept my thoughts to myself, she asked, "Why were we up north?"

"We went to help Esapett and Jon-owland keep new Cloth-men out of Koussinoc."

"How did you come to trust Esapett and Jon-owland enough to go with them so far from our own people?" Nipi asked.

"Trust came slowly, from when we first became women. Over time the trust was tested when other Cloth-men tried to harm us," I told Nipi. "Esapett and Jon-owland stood up for us many times. It was over many circles of seasons that our friendship grew strong. Your father and I went to Koussinoc to help our friends both to provide for their own and to help our people. Without the Abenaki fur trade, Esapett and Jon-owland's people would not have been able to defend us against the Narragansett and the Boston Strangers."

Nipi and Mosk were still children when we returned from living up north. Little of what we did there is told in our story songs. But the memory of how we survived seared my dreams. I did not want to speak with Nipi of the murders on the Kennebec River. Those memories would be with me as long as I lived. I did not see the killings, but the black shine of the firestick still haunted my dreams. Jon-owland had given it to Black Whale and my husband used it while we lived there, but he would have been strung up and left to die if the evil Strangers found out.

I pushed the memory away. It would be easier to give up such thoughts if I knew the end of the story. What had Esapett done with the firestick after Fish Hawk secretly returned it? Did Jon-owland still have it? If the same Boston Strangers who put Jon-alden in a cage for murder did the same to Jon-owland, would he have to admit that Black Whale had used his pistol? Would Black Whale be accused of killing the evil Hocking?

Even now, with Nipi a grown woman, I could not tell her how those dreams gripped my heart and made me fearful for my children and grandchildren. Our world had changed so much since I became a woman. Our tall trees had been cut down without enough young ones left standing. Even our friends did this. And we helped them when they asked us to kill so many beaver that the dams are almost all gone. Our streams now run too fast and carry away Mother Earth. So many of our people have been sent to the spirit world too young because of the Strangers' bad spirits. Mosk, Nipi, and Tumm'k were not afraid of our friends, but they knew to avoid other Strangers. I would not add to their fears.

I wanted Mosk and Tumm'k to become wise men and fathers of strong daughters and sons without the need to use the Strangers' firesticks. I wanted Nipi, and her daughters to serve on the Grandmothers' Caucus without having to consider sending our men to war. As long as possible, I would shield them from the increasing tides of Strangers flowing from across the Big Salt Water, bringing with them more firesticks.

Esapett and I would continue to exchange messages about our families. It could not last. Only the spirits knew when, but I was certain she would have to send a message with two arrows in a heart.

Nawhaw nessis-farewell.

1660

Elisabeth and Attitash

Owls drift slowly in the night.
Children and grandchildren fill my life.
Messages give me small comfort—grandchildren born, elders gone.
Memories of my time with her fade sometimes,
then a new message comes.
I miss my friend.

ACKNOWLEDGMENTS AND SOURCES
FOR THE INTERESTED READER

ACKNOWLEDGEMENTS

Three writers from a class at the Loft Literary Center—Rosemary Jensen, Barbara Schue, and Peter Arnstein—read every word weekly and gave me priceless advice and encouragement. My lasting gratitude to them. Nick Dimassis, an extraordinary editor, brought my story to light. Nick and his talented colleagues at Forty Press, Joe Riley, and Kelly Keady, once again did their essential magic to make a book out of my words. The more than fifty book clubs I met with provided invaluable insight. Deepest thanks to my children, Tom Vellenga, Charlotte Landreau, and Carolyn Berman, who listened to my first thoughts and last attempts to put the story into words. They and their dear spouses, Julie, Carlos, and Greg, had my back, as did my grandchildren—Stefan, Ian, Aidan, Brendan, Hannah, and Milly. All were constant in their affirmation and inspired me with their ideals, values, and talent. My sisters, Anita Cummings, and Joan McDermott provided unconditional support as did my goddaughter, Tamera Martin, and her children. My dear friends, James Morgan Johnson, Ruthena Fink, Terrie Brandt, Diane Brower Johnson, Rita Johnson , Connie Coleman, Patrick Coleman, Courtney McDonald and Morgan and Jack, as well as my new friends at Cornelia House, gave me strength and laughs, and passed my books along to others. Ada and Joseph Zepada inspired me to believe that, despite unbelievable trauma, those who have deep faith and loving friends can carry on. Joey Clark made me dig deeper and find my voice. All these friends and loved ones, as well as a host of others, kept me going during a recent hospitalization so I could recover and finish this book.

Plimoth Plantation and Hobbamock's Homesite in

Plymouth, Massachusetts made history come alive. The Minnesota Mayflower Society provided an opportunity to meet
other descendants and hear their stories. Elizabeth and John
Howland have a multitude of descendants today, including
my grandmother, Julia Jones Osborne, whose painting of a
Pilgrim woman watching the Mayflower return to England
first teased my imagination.

HISTORICAL RECORD AND HISTORICAL FICTION

*History is not just facts and events. History is also a pain in the
heart and we repeat history until we are able to make another's
pain in the heart our own.* Julius Lester

A few years before the Mayflower arrived, all the inhabitants
of Patuxet, the Wampanoag name for this area of Cape Cod,
had been captured or killed by Europeans, or died of diseases.
It had been settled by the Wampanoag many years earlier,
and who had cleared fields, grew corn, and built homes. The
new arrivals on the Mayflower did not seem troubled by the
absence of any living inhabitants. They praised God for preparing this land for them.

My first book, *Strangers in Our Midst*, portrays the first
year, 1620, during which fifty of the one-hundred Pilgrims
died. Having been saved from starvation by the Wampanoag,
the little plantation ignored this horrific winter in their letters home, instead describing a land of milk and honey in
order to bring new settlers. The descriptions of those driven
by personal gain and greed in Edward Winslow's *Good Newes
from New England*, motivated me to tell the story of opposing
views among the Pilgrims through the lives of Elisabeth and
Attitash in my second book, *In the Midst of Bounty*. By 1634,
the Plimoth villagers had a trading pact with the Abenaki
Tribe in Maine. *Tides of the Kennebec* tells the story of the
competition between Boston financiers' and Plimoth settlers'

desire for the Abenaki's trapping bounty in Maine and how Indigenous People paid the price.

Visits to Plimoth Plantation and Hobbamock's Homesite were essential for understanding life for the Wampanoag and Pilgrims depicted in *Strangers in Our Midst* and *In the Midst of Bounty*. The living history museum in Plymouth, MA, gave me the full view of life at Pilgrim Village in Plimoth Plantation. Stepping into the small huts that served as their homes and the portrayal by character actors of life at Plimoth in 1627 gave meaning to all my senses, and thus to my story.

At the same site, the Wampanoag people were invited to add their own story. They did so by insisting that Hobbamock's Homesite be its own independent site. Furthermore, refusing to perpetuate the delusion that "All the Indians have died out," the Wampanoag people remain their contemporary selves while demonstrating Wampanoag life at the time Europeans first brought families to live in Wampanoag territory. During the six visits there, I constantly had to shed my own misconceptions and assumptions. A three hour visit with the director in Indigenous Programs, Bob Charlebois was essential to my efforts to portray Attitash's people. The Wampanoag women were particularly instructive, moving me beyond my patriarchal upbringing to a matriarchal/matrilineal culture.

The original fort, *Koussinoc*, in Augusta, Maine, was replaced by Fort Western in 1754. This fort, the results of a dig from the remains of the original fort, reveal much about early settlers, as well as Abenaki people, and is now the Kennebec River Museum. With log palisades, it is still standing and well worth visiting. I am greatly indebted to the Indigenous staff at Koussinoc in Maine. When a ceremony is private to their culture, I imagined details, hoping they would be consistent with Indigenous beliefs. My apologies for any mistakes, they are mine, not theirs.

While I used the names of historical people for all Pilgrim characters and for some of the Wampanoag, I attempted to write what is plausible in addition to known historical events. For example: the known facts of the encounter between Robert Hocking and John Howland are related as faithfully as possible. Details on Moses Talbot, the man with John Howland, only reveal that he was killed. Therefore, I could imagine some events to bring life to this man who is only remembered by his death. It was tempting as an author to imagine the identity of the killer, but history is more interesting, so I stuck with speculation and guilt. In short, this is a work of historical fiction.

Little was written by about the women beyond their birth, marriage and death. The record does show the historical Elizabeth Tilley was baptized in England on August, 1607 and travelled on the Mayflower with her parents. John Howland was born in England in 1592. He was Governor John Carver's servant, probably his clerk. The dates of the births of the Howland children are as accurate as possible with a few discrepancies in records. Elizabeth Howland did bear at least ten children who grew up to bear their own children.

History also shows John and Elizabeth Howland sailing in a small shallop from Plimoth to the Kennebec River in Maine. They lived in a two-story fortress near what is now Augusta. Again, it is not of historical record that any Wampanoag accompanied the Howland group to Abenaki land, but I did not want to leave Attitash and Black Whale out of this dramatic event.

Attitash is a fictional character, as are her mother, siblings, aunts, uncles and Black Whale. The cross-cultural experience between Elizabeth and Attitash is also fiction. Although the English records do mention interaction between the Pilgrim and Wampanoag men, nothing is mentioned of women. Based on close cross-cultural friendships of my own, I am convinced such interaction between two young women is plausible. However, it was clear to me that as a non-native person, I would have difficulty understanding Wampanoag ceremonies and rituals. My Native friends here in mid-continent—Dakotah, Lakotah, Ojibwe, and Lanape—provided much insight in that regard. Many thanks to Elona Street Stewart, John Pourpot, Lavon Lee, and Professor Anton Treuer, all of whom provided patient scrutiny and vital encouragement.

English spelling was not consistent during those early years. To distinguish my imagined character from the historical person, Elizabeth Tilley, I used the spelling of Elisabeth. The spelling of the Wampanoag leader is Massasowet in Edward Winslow's writing and Massasoit in Bradford's. This word is a title meaning "honored—revered," so I often use "our Massasowet" when Attitash and other Wampanoag people speak, just as the Pilgrims describe Bradford as "our governor." The Pilgrims' view of the Native Americans is recorded using many historically negative terms, including "savages."

Following the signing of the treaty of mutual protection, the Wampanoag nation's leader, the Massasoit, asked one of his warriors, Hobbamock, to live near the new settlement to ensure that the English followed the treaty's terms. The record describes Hobbamock as bringing a large family with him. In their matrilineal society the Massasoit and Hobbamock would have followed the instructions of the Wampanoag grandmothers' caucus. This aspect of governance was lost on the Pilgrim men. They referred to the Massasoit as "king."

An excellent collection of original documents is found in the American Historical Documents volume of the Harvard Classics. These include: "Voyages to Vinland," c. 1000; "Christopher Columbus Letter," 1493 (prepare to be greatly disturbed by his descriptions of native people); "First Charter of Virginia," 1606; "The Mayflower Compact," 1620; "Fundamental Orders of Connecticut," 1639 (referred to as the first written democratic constitution by Europeans/Americans; and the "Massachusetts Body of Liberties," 1641 (of these, seventy-eight are liberties for men, four each for children and servants, and two for women).

The Mayflower, by Vernon Heaton, RAF who served in WWII, provides information about the struggles against King James which led the so-called Puritans to leave England, some of their faith having been executed, and live in Holland. Heaton describes the Puritans' desire to raise their children without the Dutch until the threat of the Spanish Inquisition coming to Holland, as well as documentation of their journey and life in the New World.

William Bradford's *Of Plymouth Plantation*, and Edward Winslow's *Good Newes from New England* and *Mourt's Relation* are primary sources written by Mayflower passengers. It is interesting to compare their accounts. The writers are all Anglo men, however, and little was written about the women. *A Little Commonwealth, Family Life in Plymouth Colony*, by John Demos, is an in-depth study of family life and child-rearing. *Good Wives* by Laurel Thatcher Ulrich and *Founding Mothers and Fathers*, by Mary Beth Norton were most helpful describing female life in Plimoth.

The Times of Their Lives, by James & Patricia Scott Deetz gives significant details about every aspect of life in Plimoth Plantation and also describes the addition of Hobbamock's Homesite to the site near Plymouth.

Facing East from Indian Country, by Daniel Richtor, an in-depth book on events of North America seen through indigenous people's point of view. *People of the First Light, Wisdoms of a Mashpee Wampanoag Elder*, by Joan Tavares Avant (Granny Squannit), is an invaluable insight into historical and contemporary experiences. (www.mashpeenwampanoag-tribe.com)

David Truer's *The Heartbeat of Wounded Knee, Native America from 1890 to the Present*, came out as I wrote this third book. It is essential to understand Indigenous People today in order to attempt to portray them four hundred years ago. Truer writes, "The how shapes the what. How we see the people, their lives, their actions, and the meanings that obtain from those lives and actions shapes the present and the possible future....I have tried to catch us not in the act of dying but, rather, in the radical action of living."

Braiding Sweetgrass, by Robin Wall Kimmerer. An invaluable view of the natural world, from the author's understanding both as a member of Citizen Potawatomi Nation and Professor of Environmental Biology. Her work reveals a rare acquaintance with our original roots.

Children's books are a source for pictures and the daily life. *Tapenum's Day*, by Kate Waters and Russ Kendall, about a Wampanoag family and their books on Pilgrim children's "day" are accurate depictions of family life at that time. *Giles and Metacom* by Pamela Dell, nicely portrays two young boys.

There are many Wampanoag websites, including www.plimoth.org/what-see-do/wampanoaghomesite.

Despite the New Englanders' attempt to annihilate the Wampanoag, they survived. The Wampanoag Nation has its tribal headquarters on the tip of Noepe, the island which English speakers call Martha's Vineyard, in the town of Aquinnah. Notably, in 1997, the town voted 79-76 to change its name from Gay Head, to Aquinnah, the area's original Native American name (*Vineyard Gazette*, 5/17/2018.)